To Dixie
An

"Trust the
Good will always come
to those who wait...

RUNAWAY

A Novel

C.A. Simonson

C A Simonson

This is a work of fiction. Names, characters, places, and incidents either are products of the author's imagination or are used fictitiously. Any resemblance to actual events or locales or persons, living or dead, is entirely coincidental.

Cover Design– C.A. Simonson

ISBN: 9781097772322

DEDICATION

This book came about originally from a dream. It had to marinate in the author's mind for many years before putting pen to paper.

I dedicate this book to those who are advocates for abused and hurting children. These people take extra time, effort, and money to help and support needy children.

As foster parents in years past, my husband and I understand the involvement and dedication needed. I commend the loving families who open their homes to foster children who simply want love and a place to call home.

The ultimate goal in writing a story such as this is to encourage the hurting, inspire the volunteers, and hopefully, to touch the reader's heart. Hope and faith are always there, but we must learn to trust the wait.

"Be strong and take heart, all you who hope in the Lord."
Psalm 31:24 (NIV)

Contents

ACKNOWLEDGEMENTS

A huge thank you goes out to my husband for encouraging me to write what's in my heart. Without his steadfast support in me as an author, I wouldn't be able to spend the hours it takes to dream, write, and create.

Thank you to Marilyn Quigley, a marvelous editor with a background as a professor in English/Literature at Evangel College. She painstakingly took my manuscript and helped with background mechanics to transform it from words into a meaningful story. Marilyn now volunteers her time with Royal Family Kids, an international organization which helps abused, abandoned, and neglected children in Springfield, Missouri.

Lastly, I am grateful to my writing group, Springfield Writers' Guild in Springfield, Missouri, for the camaraderie, support, and encouragement from fellow writers and authors.

RUNAWAY

1 - DAMAGED GOODS

Getting into the car with that man had been a bad idea. A really bad idea. He's not going the right way... and he looks at me the same way Benny did. I've got to get away!

Only a few hours earlier, the girl didn't know which way to go or where to turn. Her legs ached after walking only a few miles. Her belly growled, and she was so tired—was there any other choice? She had opened the passenger's side door and slid onto the oily-looking seat thinking the old man was being nice when he'd offered her a ride into town. Grateful for the piece of candy, she popped it into her mouth. But when he started to drive the other way, she panicked. Stealing a look at the driver out of the corner of her eye, she watched and waited for her chance to run.

His onion-smelling breath came through a few missing teeth when he ordered her to stay in the car. The odor of pumping gas along with the other funny smells in the car almost made her gag. She scooted closer to the door and waited for her chance to escape.

The old man wiped his oily hands on his pants, gave her a glare, and then went inside to pay. He glanced out the door to make sure she was still in the child-locked car and then went into the men's bathroom.

My chance. She lifted the latch, but it wouldn't move. *Oh No! Am I locked in?* Trying her best to lift the lock with her tiny fingers, it wouldn't budge. The girl peeked over the dash to see if the man had come out of the bathroom yet. With no sign of him, she quickly slid over to the driver's side, opened the door a crack, and then ducked low as she tumbled out. She ran down the dirt road as fast as her crooked leg would take her. *Stupid leg. Never works right.* Her leg twisted on some loose gravel and she sprawled onto her face. Scrambling to her knees with a quick look back, her breaths came in short pants. No sign of the old man. When she tried to stand, her ankle turned, tumbling her over and over into the nearby steep ditch. Landing in a puddle of water, she held her hand over her mouth to stifle a cry. Arms and legs scraped–but not broken. She tucked her knees up under her body and curled into a ball, pulling the garbage bag over her body as much as possible.

It started out to be such a wonderful day, but it went downhill fast. "Get out and never come back," rang in her ears. The events of this terrible day that threatened to end everything she'd ever known replayed in her mind.

Earlier that morning Nina had told her to dress up because they were going someplace–something Nina never said or did. The girl donned her favorite sundress dotted with tiny yellow flowers and washed her face. She attached a yellow satin ribbon to the side of her long black curls, satisfied the scar wouldn't show. The smell of smoked bacon drifted through her door and she followed her nose to the kitchen.

"About time you get down here, you lazy fool," Nina sounded gruff. "Hurry and eat. I have a surprise for you today." Her smile was menacing.

The girl's heart began to thump harder as she poked bacon into her mouth. *Nina's surprises were never good.* She stopped chewing. "What kind of surprise?"

"Don't question me!" Nina clenched her teeth. "Just do as I say!"

"One more bite, please?"

Nina scowled at the girl. "You've had enough. It's time to go."

"Where?" She hurried to pull on her sandals.

"Shut up and get your shoes on. Hurry."

She dodged the swipe of Nina's hand and shut her mouth. *Nina never takes me anywhere for fun.* Getting into the car, she worried even more. *Nina never takes me anywhere, period.*

Forty minutes down the road, they arrived at a two-story building by the lake called 'Benny's Place'.

"C'mon." Nina opened the door and yanked on her arm.

"Can I go by the water?"

"No."

"But I want—"

Nina raised her hand, cutting her off. "You babbling twit. I don't care what you want and if you don't shut up, I'm gonna slap you silly." Nina clamped her hands around the girl's shoulders and shook her. "You'll do exactly as I say. Understood?"

She pulled her head back as Nina began to finger-brush her long hair. Yanking the girl toward her, the older woman frowned. "Put a smile on your face and at least *try* to look pretty. I want you to meet someone." She spoke through tightened lips. "He may become a very important man in your life."

Taking a huge breath, the child sucked in the tears threatening to come and wondered who Nina knew here.

Still fit and trim for her almost fifty years of age, Nina had taken extra time to prepare herself for this reunion, excited to see Benny again.

"Benny around?" she asked with a winsome smile.

"Who's asking?" The gnarly, unshaven man kept wiping the counter and did not look up.

"An old friend. I brought someone for him."

The man glanced sideways at her and then caught a glimpse of the budding pre-teen. "Hmm...I see." He eyed the child from her from head to toe. "I'll go get him."

Hiding behind Nina, the girl trembled at the way he had looked at her. Her stomach hurt; she wanted to leave. Nina pulled her out from behind her with a rough tug and readjusted the hair ribbon.

Benny appeared with a scowl on his face but stopped short at seeing the redhead he once used as his own. "Is that you, my love?" Benny grabbed Nina around her thirty-inch waist and squeezed her close. He planted a wet kiss on her bright red lips. "Ten years, and you still look mighty fine! Always loved your red curls." Benny ran his rough hands through her boxed-red hair and then saw the girl who had moved closer to the door. Releasing his hold on Nina, he turned toward her. "And who might this be?"

Nina grabbed the girl's arm and thrust her towards Benny. "For you, Benny." Her voice took on a sickening sweetness. "Take a good look. She may be useful to you." The woman gave the girl a mild shove. "Go on now, smile for the man."

She tried her best, but no smile would come. Her eyes widened in fright. She cringed as he twirled a curl of her raven hair around his finger.

"Come, girlie," Benny crooned smoothly, taking her hand. "Turn around and let me look at you." He attempted to twirl the girl in a circle before him, but her leg would not cooperate. She stumbled and fell into Benny's arms. Face flushed and hot, she quickly pushed herself away when he stared at her leg.

He scratched his stubbled chin with a slight frown on his face. "Walk over to the wall and then come back here to me."

Puzzled, but afraid to disobey, she half-hobbled to the wall and then back to the strange man, trembling with each tiny step. Her leg throbbed.

The frown deepened. "Hmmm..." he muttered. "Come closer, girlie."

Benny took her face in his hands, tipped her chin upward and checked every feature as if examining a new workhorse. He untied the yellow ribbon and ran his stubby fingers through her thick black curls, pushing the hair behind her ears.

Heart beating wildly, she felt reduced to nothing. Her stomach hurt; she felt faint. She looked pleadingly at Nina who perched on the bar stool applying more lipstick, awaiting the final approval. *Say something, Nina*! She screamed inside.

"What's this?" He scowled, holding the curls back from her cheeks. As he pushed his finger on the ugly, jagged scar, it puffed up into a crimson welt. "You bring me damaged goods?"

"She's still a pure one," Nina defended. "She could be profitable for you."

"Won't do. She's flawed."

"The scar can be hidden. No one will notice in the dark."

"She's damaged. No man wants a scarred cripple. Her kind is forbidden here. She's only good for one thing."

"But, Benny...."

"Joe!" Benny yelled toward the kitchen. "C'mere. Take this kid to the back. You know what to do."

Benny shoved the girl toward Joe, a greasy old man with a withered face and a cigar hanging from his lips. He motioned for her to come with him. Fighting away the tears, she froze and shook her head no.

Old Joe walked over, grabbed the girl's arm and pulled her toward the back. She struggled against his gruff hold.

"Please, Nina. Don't make me. I don't want to."

But Nina's black mascaraed eyes were closed in Benny's embrace as he kissed her slender neck.

Joe shoved the girl onto the greasiest part of the kitchen floor and then kicked a bucket of water and a scrub brush toward her. "Git it clean," he ordered, flicking cigar ashes her way.

Her sundress soon became a dingy gray from

scrubbing the oily floors. Her leg ached; her back hurt; her heart worried. *When will Nina come? I want to go home.* She felt alone and afraid, and then a deeper worry arose. *Will she leave me here?*

After what seemed like hours, Nina walked into the kitchen with a scowl. "C'mon you good-for-nothing lout."

Cowering by the car window all the way home, she felt an empty hurt inside. She held back the tears by covering her eyes and sobbed in silence. Nina mumbled through clenched teeth as she steered the car toward home.

Nina's mad at me again, and I don't even know why. I'll probably get a whipping, but at least she didn't make me stay there.

Her mind jerked back to the present as she heard the car start up back at the gas station. She wanted to look, but didn't dare. She stayed still, hidden under the garbage bag shivering with fear—hoping the man wouldn't look in the ditch.

2 – DISCOVERY

LATE AFTERNOON

"Faith! Come. Quick. I need your help," Hope called to her younger sister from the drive.

Faith opened the front door to see her sister struggling with–with what? She appeared to have her large arms wrapped around something in a blanket. At the sight and frantic sound of Hope's voice, Faith hurried to meet her outside.

"What in the world are you bringing home this time?" Faith shoved her wire-framed glasses up on her nose to get a better look.

"Not a what–a who." Hope guided the small-framed child to the bench beside the front door while she caught her breath. She fanned her reddened face from the exertion and smoothed back an unruly wisp of her white hair. "Help me get her inside, and then I'll go fetch her belongings from the car."

"A child?" Faith asked in a whisper. "Who is she? Is she lost? Where did you...? How did...?"

"We'll speak later, sister. Right now we must tend to her needs."

The child peeked from beneath the blanket. *They seem kind. Should I trust them? But it was the only way for me to escape from that ugly man. I was scared to go with her...but too scared not to. They don't act mad like Nina.* She hid her head under the blanket and listened. *Maybe they'll be nice to me.* The younger one with the soft voice was speaking.

"But–where was she going? Who does she belong to?" asked the taller, thinner lady with a bit of gray in her hair. "She can't be more than twelve years old—slight little thing with hardly any meat on her."

Hope put her finger on Faith's lips to stop her sister's rant. "She's hurt and cold, Faith. Let's think about helping her right now."

"You're right, Hope. I'm letting my mouth get in the way again." She adjusted her glasses and reached toward the girl. The girl ducked her pretty oval face farther under the blanket. Surprised, Faith lowered her hand and took a step back.

When the girl tried to stand on her own, her damaged leg gave way on her broken sandal. Grabbing the bench so she wouldn't topple, she gave Faith a pleading, timid look.

"Mercy me. What big black eyes you have, child. Don't worry, I won't hurt you." Faith leaned toward her. "You're safe with us."

The girl was too exhausted to resist as Faith bent over to help her up. "Let's get you inside. I'll fix you some soup while Hope runs some water for a bath. Whatever happened to you, child?" She clicked her tongue. "Whatever it was, we'll get you fixed up. You don't have to worry none here."

"Don't be afraid," said Hope, once the girl was seated at the table. "We only want to help you."

The girl looked away, shyly pulling her long black curls over the left side of her face.

Faith set a glass of milk and a steaming bowl of soup before the quivering child. As she gulped down the food, she kept a wary eye on the ladies and one hand over her face.

Faith whispered to Hope, "She must be starved. Poor little thing."

"Appears so." Hope readjusted her long white hair into a neat bun. "When did you eat last, child?" she asked.

The girl refused to answer, keeping her eyes on the table. The ladies sat with her until she finished eating, and then Hope gave her a smile. "There. That should help. Now, come. You'll feel better after a good night's rest. I'll show you where you can lay down and sleep. But first, a bath to get you cleaned up. Are you able to get into the tub with that leg? It looks mighty painful.

And you're all scraped up, poor thing."

The girl's eyes darted about the house, taking in every detail.

"Are there pajamas in your bag?"

A slight nod.

"All right, then. The bathroom is at the end of the hall. I'll lay out your pajamas. Take your time to bathe and then rest as long as you like, my dear."

While she was in the bathroom, the ladies conversed.

"Where in the world did she come from?" asked Faith. "Her clothes are in a garbage bag, for heaven's sake!"

"I reckon I don't rightly know," said Hope. "I found her crying and trying to hide in the ditch underneath that garbage bag. Heaven be my witness! I saw the garbage bag in the ditch on my way home from the market. As I looked closer, it shocked me to see a leg sticking out from under it. I stopped to look and found this little girl shivering in fright."

"Mercy me!" said Faith. "What was she doing on the side of the road?"

"Don't know how she got there or why she was trying to hide. Maybe she sprained her ankle or something and fell. Must have been too hurt to get back up again. My heart went out to her. I just had to help her."

Faith's head wobbled in agreement. "What's her name?"

"Don't know. Hasn't spoken a word since I found her. Her tiny body was trembling, wearing only a sundress and a sweater that wouldn't keep a fly warm. Not enough clothing for these cool nights we've been having. I have no idea how long she's been outside. She seems very afraid. Wasn't sure she'd even come with me."

"It's a good thing you found her when you did, then. Maybe she'll open up and talk once she's bathed and rested."

"Do you think I should check on her? She's been in there a long time."

"No, I'm sure she's capable of bathing herself." Faith knit her brows as she put away the food and dishes. "You don't intend on keeping her here, do you? Shouldn't we call someone? She might be lost or in danger."

"We must care for her needs first, sister. Let's find out her name and hear her story first. There must be a good reason she was out there alone," said Hope.

After soaking in a hot tub, it felt good to have her body clean and her belly full. The girl crawled into bed and snuggled under the soft blanket, grateful to finally lie down. Her leg ached. She wondered what would have happened if she had stayed all night in the ditch.

The kindness of these ladies overwhelmed her, but she would be cautious; she had been tricked before. Shivering in spite of the warm covers, she turned toward the wall and let her tears spill onto the pillow. Her chest rose and fell with her sobs.

Will they treat me like Nina did, or can I trust them? I won't say a word until I know for sure. Please, don't let them think I'm good-for-nothing too.

3 - NO WORDS

The girl awoke the next morning wondering where she was. It took a few minutes to gather her senses. She didn't realize she'd been that tired.

Sitting up, she rubbed the sleep from her eyes to gaze around the room. The walls were papered with tiny yellow roses. Somehow that comforted her. A small chest of drawers sat on the other side of the room. A soft white bedspread covered the single bed, and frilly curtains framed the one window where a window seat laden with fluffy pillows beckoned her. *It all feels cheery and most of all, safe. Nothing like my room.*

Rubbing the sore spot on her leg, she remembered running from the man at the gas station. The leg still throbbed from her tumble into the ditch. The hard pit in the bottom of her stomach tied itself into another knot.

What now? I can't go home. Nina told me to never come back. The cruel words still rang in her ears. She let her body fall back onto the bed. She buried her head under the pillow and wondered where she would go. *At least those men can't find me here.* The tears began to flow again.

"You up, sweetie?" The door opened a crack as Hope stuck her head into the room. Seeing the child in tears, she went over to the bed and gathered the small bundle into her large arms, holding her close.

Maybe she really does care. The girl melted into the woman's tender embrace. *Maybe I can trust her.* She pressed her head into the woman's large bosom and sobbed. *It feels so good to be hugged.*

"There, there, now, honey, it's all right." Stroking the hair away from her eyes, Hope pulled a tissue from her pocket. "Shhhh. You're safe here."

As her weeping subsided, she quieted in Hope's arms. Nuzzling into the warmth of the hug, she held onto the large woman like an anchor in a raging storm.

Hope gave the girl one last squeeze and gently loosened her embrace. "I'm sure you must be hungry? Hmmm?" She dabbed away the tears.

She nodded without looking at Hope.

"Okay, then. When you're dressed, come down for breakfast. I'll tell my sister to get it started."

Her eyes darted about the room.

Hope patted the child's arm. "Don't worry, child. Faith washed your dress from yesterday. I put the rest of your things in the chest."

She breathed a huge sigh of relief and forced a half-smile.

"Okay, then. Get dressed." Hope rose. "We'll be waiting for you downstairs. I hope you like pancakes."

"Has she spoken yet?" Faith asked when Hope came downstairs.

"No. Poor child. Appears she sprained her ankle when she fell into the ditch–if that's what happened," Hope said.

"Where do you suppose she came from? And why would a child her age be out wandering the highway that time of day?" Faith touched her chin. "Mercy, me. Her parents must be worried sick."

"All in time, dear sister. For now, we'll give her food and shelter and let her know she's safe. Someone has hurt her deeply."

Faith gasped and put her hand to her mouth. "You don't mean...?"

"Oh! No–no, I don't mean...well, I really don't know what I mean," said Hope. "Somehow I know in my heart this girl has been hurt by someone. Maybe more than one, and deep in her soul, she's in pain. She needs our help. More than that, she needs God's healing."

"Mercy me," said Faith. "Well, we can help, can't we?"

"...and we can pray and love and care for her. Poor child," agreed Hope.

The girl limped into the kitchen looking much fresher than she had the night before. Timidly she eyed the two women. Her grimace spoke volumes as she sat down, self-consciously rubbing her hurting leg.

"You must have taken quite a spill," said Faith. "You're still limping."

The girl kept her thoughts to herself. *It's not from the fall. I've always had this stupid limp. I hate this crooked dumb leg. Is that why Nina hates me so much? Or does she hate me 'cuz I'm ugly? The devil probably kicked me in the leg when he gave me the scar.*

Faith set a plate of hot pancakes drizzled in maple syrup in front of the girl who took a deep whiff and began to eat. Hope interrupted with a chuckle. "Let's thank the Good Lord first, okay?"

The child's face reddened as she dropped her fork on the table. She bowed her head, hoping she hadn't made these ladies mad, too.

"...and last of all, we thank you, dear Lord, for this sweet child. Thank you for bringing her to us so we can help her. Help us find where she belongs. Praise be to God. Amen."

"Now, let us introduce ourselves. I'm Hope. This is

my sister, Faith. Neither of us married, so we decided to live together to keep each other company. Isn't that right, sis?"

Faith nodded. "Momma and Papa always wanted another girl so they could name her Charity."

Hope's chuckle was contagious. "But it was only us two. So, sweetie, what's your name? What shall we call you?"

Her little body tensed as she stopped eating mid-bite. She stared at the table trying to think of an answer. *I can't tell these women my name. I can't go back. No one dares know who I am or where I came from.* She pushed a huge bite of pancakes into her mouth, refusing to look them in the eye.

Faith clucked and gave Hope a wondering gaze. They had touched a nerve. Hope looked around the room. Her eyes landed upon a vase of fresh roses sitting on the table. She viewed the timid, shaking child before them.

"How about if we call you Rose? Would that name work?"

Her black eyes widened as she arched her eyebrows. Beginning to choke on her food, she took a drink of her milk, and gave a slight nod.

"Rose it is, then. Maybe Rosie for short?" Hope's eyes lit up when she saw a tiny smile form on the girl's lips. "Yes. Rosie. It suits you, sweetie. You're as beautiful and delicate as this red rose."

"And I'll bet just as sweet," Faith added.

The girl's cheeks flushed a warm pink. *Yep. I like these ladies.*

4 - RUNAWAY?

A couple of days passed as Rosie settled into the routine of Faith and Hope Abrams. Rising early, she gladly helped with anything she was asked to do. Faith tried in desperation to get the girl to talk asking all kinds of questions, but she held her tongue, refusing to utter a sound.

"Thank you for your great help in setting the table. Now, what should we make for breakfast? Any ideas?"

Rosie only shrugged each time, nodded or shook her head—but her inhibitions began to dissolve under the sisters' gentle care. She had never known anyone as kind and loving. They made her feel like she belonged, and she hoped it could stay that way forever. After eating a bowl of oatmeal, Rosie took her bowl to the sink, ready to start washing dishes.

"It's a gorgeous day," said Faith, opening the window. "Why not go sit in the garden? Enjoy some sunshine."

Rosie opened the screen door, breathed in the fresh air, and blinked in the bright sunlight. The warm concrete bench close to the rose bushes radiated its heat on her bottom. She tipped her face upward and let the sun's ray beat on her face. *It feels so good to be free and safe...and wanted.*

Hope yawned widely as she shuffled into the kitchen in her robe and slippers, her white shoulder-length hair askew. As she set the teapot on to boil, she noticed Faith looking out the window. "What's on your mind, sis?"

"Our girl doesn't act like she's lost. Do you think she ran away from home? Or do you think someone dumped her by the side of the road?"

"I would hate to think..." Hope didn't finish the horrible thought as she eased herself onto a chair.

Faith poured them both cups of tea and joined Hope at the table. "She had all her belongings, what little there was, in that garbage bag. A couple of sundresses, pajamas, underwear, and..." she paused, "...and a beautiful gold scarf. It seemed so out of place with the other plain things."

"But if she ran away, who would she be running from, and where would she be going?"

"What if she stole the scarf?" Faith scratched her graying head for a clue. "If she's a thief, she would want to run and hide."

Hope rose to put her cup in the sink and looked out the window. Rosie was gently pulling weeds around the rose bushes. “A couple of days, and you put her to work already?”

“A little dirt under her nails is good for the soul; the sunshine refreshes the body, and it might brighten her spirit, too.”

“You have a way with words,” sighed Hope.

“But so you know, I didn’t put her to work. I told her to go outside and enjoy the sunshine. It was her choice to pull weeds.”

“Well, she seems content here,” said Hope.

“Someone must be looking for her. How will they know where to look if we don’t tell anyone?”

“We can’t hurry her healing process. Rest will do her leg and her body good. Plus,” Hope pulled the thought from her heart. “We still don’t know her name yet. She needs time.”

They sat a few moments in reflection.

“Hope...” Faith scratched her nose. “Did you see that awful-looking scar on her face?”

“I noticed it the first night. That’s not from falling into the ditch. That’s an old wound.” Hope wagged her head. “What else has this poor child suffered?”

“Perhaps we should take her to the doctor. Get her checked out. She still limps and appears to be in pain with each step.”

“I suppose you’re right,” Hope hedged.

“I’ll call and make an appointment. Maybe he can

persuade her to talk to us."

"What if she's not able to speak?"

"Well, it's clear she's not deaf," said Faith, "she hears and understands us just fine."

A couple of days later, Faith broke the news to Rosie. "Tomorrow, Rosie, we're taking you to the doctor for a checkup on that leg."

Rosie's expression turned to horror. She began to twist her hair in her fingers.

"Sweet girl, you're still limping. You're still hurting. That leg of yours should have healed by now. Maybe he can see what's wrong and make it better. He can check to see if it's sprained or if there's a fracture from your fall."

"N-n-no! No! No!" Rosie whimpered in barely a whisper. She hobbled as fast as she could up the stairs, with her hands over her ears.

Faith and Hope looked at one another with open mouths.

"So. She *can* speak," Faith said.

"Hmmmm...." pondered Hope with her hands on her abundant hips. "Whatever is troubling that child, we must help her get to the root of it."

"If it's not buried too deep," said Faith. "It's evident she's afraid of something..."

"... or someone," finished Hope.

5 - DOCTOR VISIT

It took a lot of gentle persuasion on Hope's part, and bribery on Faith's behalf to get Rosie into the car and to the doctor's office.

"I'm glad you could fit us in on such short notice, Dr. Edwards," said Faith. "I realize you're not a pediatrician, but perhaps you could take a look at our girl."

"And who do we have here?" asked the doctor.

"We've named her Rosie, but we don't really know who she is. She won't speak. She took a bad fall last week and still limps. We thought she may have sprained her ankle, or worse. It hasn't improved even though we've had her resting all week."

"Hmm-hmm," he said, wrinkling his forehead at the ladies. "All week, you say?" Facing Rosie, he asked, "Can you hop up on the table for me, Miss?"

Rosie gave Hope a pleading stare, shaking her head.

"It's okay, Rosie. He won't hurt you."

"Stay with me?" Her tiny voice was laced with fear.

Both women's eyes blinked in surprise at hearing her speak.

“Of course, sweetie,” said Hope, “come on.” Hope helped her up onto the examining table and patted her arm. “I’ll be right over here.”

“That’s the first real sentence we’ve heard her speak in five days.” She whispered to Dr. Edwards as she passed him.

Dr. Edwards did the usual routine of exams and then pursed his lips. “Umm-hmmm. Okay, Miss Rosie. I think we’re done here.”

Getting down off the table, she stumbled. The doctor grabbed her arm to support her as she regained her balance on the floor.

“Sorry,” she muttered, her tiny voice barely audible. Giving him a shy look, she rubbed her bum leg.

“Tell me. Does your leg always hurt?”

Rosie gritted her teeth and gave him a slight nod.

“How long has it been this way?”

She shrugged her shoulders.

“Has it been like this since you were little?” he asked further.

She nodded.

“How did you hurt it?”

She gave him an ‘I-don’t-know’ look.

“How about the scar on your face? Has it always been there too?” he asked.

“Uh-huh.”

The doctor nodded with no emotion. "Were you born with it?"

She tucked her chin and shrugged her shoulders.

He glanced at the women with knowing concern. "Ladies, I'm going to have to x-ray her leg."

Rosie shook her head, her eyes large. "Why?"

"It's okay, Rosie," Hope put her arm around the girl. "An x-ray doesn't hurt."

"Come with me?" she pleaded.

Hope looked to the doctor for approval. "Sure, honey. But we'll have to stand outside the door."

They went to the Radiation Department where the procedure was performed. While they waited for results, Hope and Faith conversed in hushed voices as Rosie watched television.

Faith picked up a magazine and leafed idly through the pages without looking at them. "You know he thinks that scar is more than a birthmark."

"Well, I think she's been through something awful. Hopefully, we'll find out something soon."

Dr. Edwards came back into the room. "I need to talk to you ladies privately. Rosie, can you stay here while we talk in the other room?"

She shook her head. "No, please. Don't leave me alone."

"I'll wait out here with you, honey," Hope said. "Faith, you talk to the doctor. You can fill me in later."

On the way home, Rosie surprised both women by talking nonstop.

"Thanks for the ice cream," Rosie said from the back seat. "I love vanilla."

Faith gave Hope an optimistic look and nodded. "You were a brave girl today, Rosie. We make good on our promises." She took a lick of her cone. "We thought ice cream might make your day even better. Now, we're taking you to the mall to look for a new Sunday dress."

Rosie grinned, wondering what was so special about Sunday. This kind of affection was all so new. "Can it be red?"

"Like a red rose?" chuckled Hope. "Of course. We'll find you the prettiest red dress there.

Rosie settled contently back in her seat. *I love to hear Hope laugh. I'm going to take a chance and trust them. They're nice.* "My name..." She paused as if having second thoughts. She began again with slow deliberation. "My name really *is* Rose."

"Well, well. We chose a good one then, didn't we?" Hope's laugh was full of joy.

"Rose. Rose, what? What's your last name, Rosie?" questioned Faith.

"Rosie Dela—," she stopped short. *I don't dare tell them that much. They may send me back, and what will I do then?* "Uh...just Rosie." She scooted back in her seat and pulled her knees up to her chest.

Hope turned to give her sister a stern frown and a shake of her head. “Don’t scare her off,” she whispered.

Faith drew her lips into a grimace and then mouthed an apology. “Okay, ‘just Rosie’,” she tried to mend the offense and turned around to face the girl. “Your name fits you well, you know? You look like a rose with those beautiful cheeks that blush just the right shade of pink, and they’re velvety-soft like a soft rose. The bloom on your face is framed by your thick black curls.”

Rosie blushed at the flattery, subconsciously pulling her hair over the scar that always seemed to bulge and redden when she was embarrassed.

“I wish I had gorgeous black hair like you! It would look pretty in braids tied with ribbons.”

A little frown creased Rosie’s forehead as she shook her head. *Braids? Nina always brushed my hair too hard and pulled my braids too tight.*

“I used to wear braids,” Rosie said softly, “but it made my head hurt. I don’t like braids anymore. They’re for little girls.”

“Okay, sweetie,” Faith soothed. “No braids, no worries. You’re beautiful just the way you are.”

Faith’s soft voice calmed her. *Beautiful? Nina always told me I was ugly.* She felt safe with these ladies. She relaxed and crossed her legs. They rode in silence the rest of the way to the mall while Rosie's thoughts turned back to her life with Nina and how she used yank hard on the stubborn knots in her hair. Her head used to ache with every strand of hair being pulled into submission and then secured with a thick, plain rubber band.

I hated those awful braids. The harsh words spilled back into her brain. *You stubborn oaf!*

She wasn't sure if Nina meant the braids or her....

6 – QUESTIONS

"Thank you for all these new clothes," Rosie beamed as they gathered the packages from the car.

"Our pleasure, sweetie. Go try on your new dress. See if it fits," Hope encouraged.

When she was sure Rosie was out of earshot, Hope settled heavily onto the chair in the kitchen. Faith started the coffee to brew and then sat down across from her.

"You were quite the chatterbox on the way home, sister. I was afraid the girl would clam up for good. We must go slooow," Hope emphasized the last word.

Faith lowered her voice as she spoke. "I know. I know. I'm just so full of questions since talking to the doctor. Questions only Rosie can answer."

"Well, tell me what he said. I can't wait to hear what the doctor told you!"

"First of all, Dr. Edwards asked me where Rosie came from."

"What did you say?" Hope sat owl-eyed, drumming her fingers on the table.

"I couldn't lie. He knows we have no daughters or nieces. Plus, she looks nothing like us." Faith got up to cut herself a slice of cake. "Want a piece?"

Hope grinned. “You know I never turn down cake,” Hope laughed. She patted her tummy. “Probably should. So, what did you tell him?”

“The truth. I said we’re trying to find out where she came from and that she hadn’t spoken a word until today. He asked exactly how long we’ve had her with us, and I told him a few days.”

“Close to a week,” corrected Hope, stuffing chocolate cake into her mouth.

“He said we should have contacted Child Protective Services or the police the first thing. If she ran away from home, her parents would need to know she’s been found,” Faith wagged her index finger at her sister. “Told you so, Hope.”

“You’ve also seen the fear in her eyes any time we mention leaving her, and surely social services would try to take her away. She couldn’t handle it.”

“Yes–but you also know we can’t keep her. Someone must be worried sick about her....” Faith trailed her words.

Licking the chocolate frosting from her fingers, Hope lifted herself off the chair to get another cup of coffee. “Well, that’s what we must find out. But right now, tell me. What did the doctor say about her leg?”

Faith leaned her head forward to whisper. “It’s not a sprain...or a fracture.” She grinned watching her sister fidget in suspense.

"That's good to know–but why does she limp? Why is she in pain?" Hope poured them both a refill.

"He said her left leg is twisted, barely noticeable to the eye. He had suspected she broke the leg when she was young. Either it wasn't set right, or it wasn't set at all, so it grew twisted and a little shorter."

"Then," Hope pondered, putting her finger to her chin, "...that's why he asked her if it always hurts."

They quieted their voices when Rosie came down the stairs in her new dress. "I love my new dress!" She admired herself in the hall mirror.

"It fits perfectly." Hope said.

"And it brings out the beauty of your black hair and eyes," said Faith.

Rosie tried to curtsy, but it came out as a clumsy bow. "I'm so happy! I'm going to go try on everything!"

The ladies waited for her to go back upstairs and then continued.

"Remember, Rosie said she didn't know when she hurt her leg. The x-ray proved it had been broken and healed crooked over time. It's clear she favors that leg and walks on the outer side of her foot."

"So, it had to be when she was very young. Hmm... that also explains why she would have easily lost her footing and fallen. I wonder how she broke it in the first place? Dropped as a baby? Abused? ...and what about the ugly scar on her face? Had to have been quite a deep gash. What has that girl been through?" Hope shuddered.

"My mind is reeling with a million and one questions. The doctor figured she got the scar the same time as the broken leg–maybe eight to ten years ago. Dr. Edwards knows she's here, but how do we keep others from knowing we have her? More cake?"

"Really, I shouldn't. But, oh why not? It's really good, sis." She took a forkful to her mouth. "Maybe Pastor Jim will give us advice. I'm going to invite him for dinner on Sunday, so we can ask what he thinks. His wife is out visiting her parents, so it would be confidential between him and us."

"Do you think it's wise to tell him about Rosie?"

"He's trustworthy and honest. He will give us God's wisdom. I'd much rather have him knowing about our secret house guest before the police or social services. Remember that little Wilson girl a few years back?"

"The one who kept running away from home?" asked Faith.

"Yes, that one. After Social Services got her, the judge sent her back to her abusive father. We read in the newspaper how she died from a cruel beating. They suspected her father, but it never could be proven. I couldn't bear knowing we did the same thing to Rosie. What if they sent her back to a terrible home?"

The sisters discussed and argued back and forth about what to do. They knew what was right legally, but deep in their hearts, they also knew what was right morally.

"All I know is that we have to help this child, no matter what," said Hope.

Deep in thought, Faith refilled their cups for the third time. "The doctor also asked if we thought she was a runaway. I really wish we knew, Hope. Why haven't we heard any news of a missing child on the news?"

"I'm worried too."

"You would think—" Hope stopped speaking when Rosie came into the kitchen.

"I'm hungry. May I have something to eat?" Rosie asked.

Hope rose from the table and gave her a big squeeze. "Well, yes you can, Missy. My goodness! We've been chattering for quite a spell."

"...and gobbling down cake, too. I'll get you a piece, even though dinner's right around the corner. You know, Hope, I'll have to make a whole new cake if we're having company on Sunday."

"What you guys talking about?" asked the inquisitive child. She could tell they were talking about her. *Please don't let them find out about Nina. I like it here too much.*

7 - THE GOLD SCARF

Rosie woke up Sunday morning nervous about this church idea. Hope and Faith wanted her to be their guest and said they went every Sunday. *Wonder what they do there? Nina never took me to church. I hope they won't make fun of me.*

Easing herself out of bed, she considered her options. If she pretended to be sick, she wouldn't have to go, but she didn't want to make them mad, or disappoint them either. *I guess it won't hurt to go with them -just this once.*

She pulled the red dress from the closet and laid out her beloved gold scarf on a whim. Church seemed a proper place for it. She fingered the smooth satin ribbon around its edges. It still held a light perfumed scent and was so soft to the touch.

The image in the mirror told her the ladies were right. The red dress *did* look nice with her black curls. Draping the scarf around her shoulders, she thought the gold scarf looked good too, but it also brought back memories of the day she'd found this treasure. An involuntary tremble shook her body as bad memories about the beautiful wrap mingled with the good ones. The words still stung as her mind drifted back to that day. Nina's icy words screamed in her head: *Leave. I don't want you.*

Not even Nina had known of her hiding place upstairs. Rosie was told the attic was off limits. Forbidden. Only a few months before, she dared to explore knowing Nina never went upstairs anymore. It was perfect. Rearranging a few boxes into makeshift stools, she could sit by the window and daydream, her favorite thing to do. She rubbed a spot of dirt off the crusted-over window to allow a few rays of sunshine to break through.

She had found her own private sanctuary: a secret hiding place where she could be alone with her thoughts and away from abuse. Rosie was aware she would get a whipping if she was ever caught upstairs, but at that moment, she didn't care. This was her own spot, safely tucked away from the monster who complicated her life.

One day as she sat by the window, she caught the image of a girl staring back at her from the cracked upright mirror. She turned her face to the right and then the left to get different views, but no matter how she turned, her reflection was disappointing.

Why do I have to look like this? Tracing her finger over the old scar, it bulged into a reddened welt. *'You're cursed with HIS mark.'* Rosie winced as Nina's unforgiving words echoed in her head.

Looking again at her image in the mirror, she caught a glimmer of a shiny object in the opposite corner of the attic. It beckoned her to explore. Curious, she followed the glint of light to where it danced off the metal band of an old wooden trunk. She blew off the top layers of dust and tried to lift the lid. It resisted at first, but with a little wiggling, it finally surrendered. The odor of mothballs overcame her senses.

Digging through the smelly pile of old clothes, she discovered a wrapped shirt-sized box. Her heart pounded as she lifted it out with care, sensing it might be something special. Breathless, she removed the wrapping careful not to make too much noise. Quietly lifting the lid, she discovered the most beautiful, soft scarf that seemed to float into her lap as she picked it up–a wrap woven with the finest of golden threads. The sunlight made the luxurious fibers dazzle in brilliance. Rosie traced her finger over the soft ribbon edging. Strange how the scarf had no musty odor, as if it were brand new and never used. She held it to her face, nuzzled in its softness, and sniffed the light sweet aroma of perfume. This treasure seemed magical.

"Rosie! Where are you, you lazy fool?" Nina shouted from below.

Her skin crawled at Nina's screech. Punishment would be harsh if she were found in this forbidden zone.

Fearing the dark hole, Rosie quickly shoved the scarf back into its box and stuffed it in the corner by the window. She scampered down the stairs as quickly and quietly as her hurting leg would allow, hoping she would find Nina before Nina found her.

"Rosie?" The voice came from below. Jolted back to the present, she jerked in alarm, but this wasn't the harsh voice of the past. It was the cheerful sound of a lady who cared and the happy place she'd found with the Abrams'.

She scrunched her shoulders tight, feeling secure under the softness of the scarf's folds. The scarf had always been a comfort, even on that last day. She was glad she took it.

"Ready yet, sweetie?" called Hope again.

"Coming...."

Hope and Faith eyed Rosie as she came down the stairs, shoulders encircled within the gold scarf.

"Well, well...don't you look pretty, Miss Rosie in your new red dress," said Faith.

Rosie smiled uneasily, shrugging off the compliment. "Will they make fun of me there?"

"No, no, my dear child. Everyone will love you there, you'll see," said Faith.

"Oh!" said Hope with a last-minute thought. "Wait

here. I have the perfect ribbon for your hair." She ambled to her bedroom and soon returned holding a lovely red satin ribbon. "May I?"

The girl nodded but pulled her head back a little as Hope touched her hair.

"Don't worry–no braids," Hope chuckled. "I'll be kind."

Rosie relaxed under Hope's gentle hands and then smiled when she saw what she had done. The ribbon was brought up under her raven black hair and tied into a neat small bow on top. Swooping her hair in front over the left side of her face covered her scar perfectly.

"Ooooh, I like it," she said, admiring herself in the mirror.

"Praise be. You're beautiful, child."

"That's a very lovely scarf, too," commented Faith.

Hope gave Faith a sideways glance, but Faith forged ahead anyway. "Where did you get such an expensive wrap?" Faith rubbed a corner of the scarf between her fingers.

Faith's hazel eyes seemed to read her thoughts. Caught off-guard, Rosie spoke with sarcasm before she could catch herself. "It was Nina's. Now it's mine."

"Who's Nina?" Faith asked without thinking.

Rosie's face went dark. Her lips pursed, and a frown creased her forehead. "Someone who told me she never wanted to see me again." Rosie caught a glimpse of her face in the mirror. Her angry reflection stared back at her. She didn't want to be *that* girl.

Faith raised her eyebrows at her sister and clucked her tongue.

Rosie straightened her posture as much as possible, puffed out her cheeks with air, and then blew it out slowly. "Whew." Readjusting the scarf around her shoulders, she forced herself relax. "I'm ready for church now. Just don't let anyone make fun of me, okay?"

"You're going to love Pastor Jim," Hope said desiring to change the mood and the topic as they followed their protégé out the door.

8 – CHURCH

Shepherd's Creek Church was one of the oldest churches in town. Rosie stopped at the entrance to look up at the large steeple with its lit-up cross on top. *It almost reaches the sky.*

"Welcome to our church," said Faith's friend as they stepped into the sanctuary. "A relative?"

"Our special guest," Faith replied. "This is Rose."

"We're glad you're here, Rose." The lady gave her a warm smile and squeezed her hand.

Rosie settled into the pew next to Faith and Hope, eager to see what this church thing was all about. People walked around shaking hands, greeting each other. Music playing in the background made her feel good inside. Light gleaming through the beautiful stained-glass windows caught the fibers of her scarf making it sparkle like real gold. She was about to turn to show Hope when Hope got up from her seat to go to the piano. Rosie's mouth dropped open when the light shone behind the lady's head. *Hope glows like an angel.*

She didn't know any of the songs, so she sat back, closed her eyes, and drank it all in. The music made her feel as if she was wrapped in a warm blanket, safe and unafraid. The man they called Pastor Jim got up after the singing was done. He seemed to know everything there was to know about God. He talked about a boy who ran away. She was glad to find out his father waited for him every day until he came home. *I wish I had a father and a place to call home.* Pastor Jim also talked about a lamb who had strayed away. He said Jesus was the Good Shepherd and searched for that lost lamb until it was found. Rosie fidgeted. *I feel lost too.*

"Well? What did you think of the service, Rosie?" Faith asked as she steered the car toward home.

She thought a minute. "He has a deep voice, and he sounds really smart. And I loved the music. Made me feel so good inside! I wish I could play the piano like you, Hope."

Hope turned around to face the girl in the backseat. "Maybe someday you will."

"Thank you, ladies, for inviting me to dinner today. It is perfect timing with my Mary out of town for the weekend."

"It was a wonderful message, Pastor," said Faith as she served the minister another piece of ham. "More potatoes?"

"Yes, please. And these honey buns are amazing. You're a wonderful cook, Faith."

Faith blushed. “Mercy me. Please help yourself to another.”

“Where you do think I get my fabulous figure, Pastor?” quipped Hope, patting her bulging waistline and taking another bun. Her laughter filled the room. “So, what about you, Rosie? What did you like best about Pastor Jim’s sermon?”

“I liked the part about the lost lamb,” Rosie said. “I was worried he wouldn’t be found, or that something bad would happen.”

“We are like that lamb, Rosie. Everyone is lost until the Good Shepherd finds them. He wants to bring everyone into a safe place with Him.”

“Like Hope and Faith brought me here?”

His deep laugh reassured her. “In a way. But God’s safe place is even better. He covers you and keeps you safe forever. It’s as if you’re hidden beneath His wings.”

She gave him a quizzical look, and then her eyes brightened. “Oh. Like when I wrap my scarf around me tight and it makes me feel safe.” She stuffed the last bite of bread in her mouth and then asked to be excused.

“So...,” Pastor Jim paused, waiting until the television came on in the other room. “What are you two going to do about this child? You said she’s been here for over a week?” He gave them a slight scowl and wagged his finger at them. "You do know you should have reported this right away. And if you don't call Child Protective Services tomorrow, I will."

"Told you so, Hope," said Faith.

"But she is doing so well here. She's taken to us and we're learning more about her every day," said Hope.

Pastor Jim gave them a stern look. "She belongs to someone, somewhere. People must be looking for her."

"We only want the best for her. This morning she said no one wants her, but we do. We already love her, and we'll keep her safe. We still don't know her last name or where she came from."

Faith picked it up. "We don't know if she ran away or if she was dumped like a stray pup. All we really know is she was headed toward town. We're trying to get her to tell us her story, but she clams up whenever we try. We need time. The slightest mention of her past makes her have a stomachache."

"Please, Pastor. Give us a couple more days to work with her," said Hope. "Having a child in our home has added so much to our lives already...and honestly, it will be hard to give her back."

"If there's even someone to give her back to...," finished Faith out loud.

"God can work miracles; that is a fact, and we can pray. But you must also follow the laws of the land. I know you will do the right thing, ladies."

"Thank you for your advice, Pastor," said Hope as she walked the minister to the door. "We'll ask the Lord for guidance. Thanks again for coming."

Hope entered the living room thinking Rosie would be glued to the television. Instead, she found her sitting on the piano bench in front of the old upright piano toying with the keys.

"Hope, you played piano really good this morning. Can you teach me?"

"Of course, dear. It's easy. Look," she pointed to a key. "This is 'middle C' and this," she walked her fingers up the next eight keys, "is called a C scale. Now you try."

Rosie easily placed her fingers on the keys and played the scale as shown.

"See there? You've had your first lesson." She gave the girl a squeeze.

Rosie nuzzled into her warmth.

"Hope?"

"Yes, Rosie?"

"I want to be loved by God, but—does He even know me?"

"Sweet child, He knows everything about you and every step you take. He loves you. In fact, I think He sent me along your path to find you when I did—to save you from a cold night or even worse. The best part is that we got to meet you."

"Maybe." She stared at the keys a few seconds. "Hope?

"Yes?"

"If God knows me, how can I know Him?"

Hope breathed a silent prayer thanking God for the child's innocent faith. She looked at Rosie with tenderness. "Just talk to God like you're talking to me. Tell Him how you feel. Ask Him to help you."

Rosie pondered those words, running her fingers up the scale. "Hope?"

"Yes, dear?"

"You've given me hope today." She giggled at her own pun. "Thank you for letting me stay here."

"Rosie." She took the girl's chin in her large hands, "I want you to know something. Days ahead may get tough and be hard, but never forget this: God has a special plan for your life. You'll have to hold on to faith."

"A special plan?" Rosie's eyes were wide with curiosity.

"Trust that you will find the one He has for you."

As Hope left the room, she heard Rosie practicing the scale. This child was safe and happy and there was nothing Hope wouldn't do to keep it that way, no matter what.

9 - WHO IS NINA?

"You look mighty cheery this Monday morning!" Faith greeted the pre-teen as she bounced into the kitchen.

"I *am* happy today." Her eyes brightened.

"What makes you so happy?"

"God. I talked to Him last night, like Hope said. I think He filled my happy hole where it used to be empty."

Faith clapped her hands together. "A very good way to say it. Want to help me fix breakfast?"

As they prepared eggs and bacon, Rosie asked Faith about Hope's piano playing. "I wish I could play like Hope." Rosie said as she set the table.

"Maybe she will teach you. Hope says all you do is find the song in your head and then send it to your fingers. Your fingers find the keys, and you close your eyes and let them play." She filled plates for each of them. "Pooh. Never worked for me."

Rosie hummed softly as they washed dishes after breakfast.

Faith built up her courage enough to broach the subject. "Rosie...." She handed her a dish to wipe.

"Um-hmmm?"

"Who is Nina? An aunt?"

The humming stopped abruptly. She put the unwiped dish on the counter. Her mood chilled. "Someone who hates me. Kicked me out."

Faith guarded her reaction. "Your mother?"

Rosie shook her head; her smile had disappeared.

"Your grandmother?"

Rosie wadded the dish towel up and threw it on the counter. "She's a mean woman, and I hate her."

Faith put her hand to her mouth at the reaction. With a calm, soft voice she soothed, "I'm only trying to help you, but we need some answers. We love having you here with us. You bring new life to old ladies like Hope and me."

"Who's an old lady?" Hope bantered, entering the kitchen with sleep still in her eyes, her bedhead hair hanging on her shoulders.

"You slept late and missed a tremendous breakfast of eggs and bacon, sister," Faith chided. "Now you'll have to fix your own."

"I'll fix you something," Rosie interrupted, hoping her talk with Faith was over. "Faith is done talking."

"Oh," Hope laughed. "Faith does this to me all the time. I only want my usual. Tea and toast. You're sweet for asking, though. On second thought, you can make my toast if you want."

"We were in the middle of talking about Nina,"

Faith said, bringing a downcast look to Rosie who popped some bread into the toaster.

Hope bobbed her head and groaned. “Oh Faith, you’re relentless.”

“So...” Faith took a deep breath and continued to press, “you lived with Nina, right?”

“Yeah.” Rosie refused to look at Faith. She got the butter from the cupboard and a knife from the drawer.

“Won’t she be worried about you?”

“No. Doesn’t want me. Told me to leave. Shoved me out the door – hard. Said she didn’t love me. Said to never come back.” Her words tumbled out so fast she couldn’t stop them.

Faith wagged her head. “She...she really said that?”

Rosie nodded with her head down.

“Where is she now?”

The child shrugged, refusing to look at the women. *Well, I really don’t know. The last thing I knew, she was driving away.* She buttered the toast and put it on a plate for Hope. “Do you want jelly or honey with your toast?”

“Honey, please, honey,” said Hope.

“Where’s your home?” Faith pushed further.

As Rosie reached for the honey on the top shelf, her leg suddenly felt as if it would give way. She began to topple and grabbed the counter edge to balance herself. Then she limped to the nearby chair and sat. *How much should I tell? If they find Nina, they might send me back...but if Nina's not home anymore....*

She laid her head in her hands. "We lived at a place with roses like yours."

"But, *where*, child?" Faith persisted. Hope rolled her eyes.

"Abbotsville." Her shoulders sagged in response.

"Rosie," Hope stroked her arm. "Please help us to help you, okay? Does Nina have another name? What do other people call her?"

"Rusty," her soft voice was barely audible, her eyes glued to the table.

"Rusty? What is her last name? Is it the same as yours?"

The girl avoided the question and clamped her lips tight.

"Rosie?" Faith pushed.

"Please, may I be excused? My stomach hurts," Rosie lied.

Hope nodded and then gave Faith a frown. They watched Rosie shuffle to her room without the happy face she came in with earlier.

"What now?" Faith asked her sister.

"Well, we learned that Nina's real name is Rusty and they live in Abbotsville, but it's certainly not much to go on," said Hope.

"There's still so much we don't know. How is this Nina is involved? I only hope we didn't push her too far."

"WE? YOU, dear sister. You're the one who's crossing the line."

In another town several miles away, Rusty's tangled thoughts set her heart in turmoil. '*Get rid of the kid, Rusty*', Benny had said. '*Ditch her, and you can come back here. You were good for the business. It will be like old times. Work your stuff. You know what to do. You know you want to....*'

She remembered seeing Rosie in her rearview mirror, paralyzed stone stiff in the middle of the road. She shook it off. *Well, I got rid of the kid and he took me back. What now*?

10 - FOUND OUT

The doorbell rang before lunch followed by three brisk raps on the door.

"Who would be calling at this time of the morning?" asked Faith.

She opened the door to find a lady in her mid-thirties, smartly dressed in a business suit, hair pulled back into a French twist. She held a briefcase in her hand with a large, expensive-looking leather bag flung over her shoulder.

"Hello. Ms. Abrams?"

"Yes. What can I do for you?"

"My name is Stacey Anders. I'm with the Child Protective Services of Ridgetown. I understand you are harboring a young girl at your home. Correct?"

Faith took a step back in surprise. "Hope?" She turned to call toward the kitchen. "Hope? Come quickly. We have a problem."

Hope showed Ms. Anders to their living room while Faith offered her a cup of tea. The lady refused. She found a place on the couch to sit, opened her briefcase, and pulled out several clipped papers. "I came here on business, ladies. Where is the girl now?"

Her crisp tone held no emotion as she surveyed the ladies' home.

The women exchanged worried looks. Hope wrung her hands as Faith twisted the cross necklace she wore.

"Uh...." Hope hesitated.

"You can't hide her, Ms. Abrams. I know she's here. And, I could charge you both with kidnapping, harboring a runaway, or worse. You are most fortunate I came alone today instead of bringing the police with me."

"Oh! My!" Hope gasped. "But I...we...were only trying to help the girl. Not...certainly not...kidnap her."

"Her parents may have a different story to tell," said Ms. Anders.

"I don't think she has any parents," Faith offered.

"And how do you know that?"

"She told us."

"You know you can't trust anything a runaway says."

Hope furrowed her brow. "How do you know she's a runaway?"

Ms. Anders ignored the question. "You may as well tell me everything you know because I *will* find out. And again, I'll call the police if you don't tell me," she warned.

"How? How did you even know about Rosie? Or that she was here at our home?" Faith asked, her voice coming out in a tiny squeak. "Did Pastor Jim call you?"

"No. If he knew, he was obligated to relay that information to the Child Protective Services immediately." She jotted a note in her notebook. "I found out about the girl you call Rosie from Dr. Mark Edwards. It was also his responsibility under penalty of law to call us. He suspected she was a runaway and possibly even abused. He said you've been holding this girl here for over a week."

"Well...you wait just a minute now," Hope's ire raised. "We weren't *holding* her, as you say, and certainly not against her will. I found her. She was hurting, cold, wet, and alone. We only gave this poor girl food and shelter until she felt better. We've kept her safe and were trying to find out her name and where she belonged. We've been waiting for her to tell us her story, and she's coming around."

"You know," Faith jumped in. "We haven't hidden her. She's been in plain sight all the time. She needed us to help her in her time of need. We only protected her because she was terrified. She needed to feel safe in case someone bad was after her. She didn't speak for the first four days. We thought she may be mute."

The sisters went on to explain how Hope found Rosie.

"All the more reason to call the authorities, ladies," the social worker scolded.

"She kept limping, so we thought it best to get her leg checked out by a doctor, in case she broke it."

"Honest, Ms. Anders. It took several days to learn her name is Rose. Only a few minutes ago did we learn she lived in Abbotsville with someone named Nina. Someone who, by her own words, kicked her out and told her not to come home," said Hope.

"I know it's hard to believe. What kind of person would shove a young girl out into the world with only a garbage bag full of clothes, no money, and no food? But that's the full truth," added Faith, "so help me, God."

"Children will say anything if they're runaways. They are great storytellers," said Ms. Anders without a blink. "And just to be clear, ladies. It is *my* job to dig into the details and find out where Rosie belongs, not yours. Tell me, does this 'Nina' have a real name?"

"She said it was Rusty. That's all we know."

Ms. Anders wrote the name on her paper and clipped it to a few other papers in her briefcase. "Where is Rosie now?"

Hope yielded. "Upstairs in her room."

"Take me to her. I need to speak to her–alone."

"She may not talk to you at all," warned Hope as she led her up the staircase and down the hall. "She shivers like a beaten pup when people prod her with questions she doesn't want to answer. I believe this girl has gone through something horrible–something she cannot talk about to anyone. It's taken a long time for my sister and me to draw her out as much as we have. Please, don't ruin that for us. Don't scare her away."

Ms. Anders gave the woman a stern glare. "I am a professional, Ms. Abrams. I know my job and I know what I'm doing."

Hope opened the door a crack to Rosie's room. The girl sat in the window seat rocking back and forth, surrounded by pillows. Gazing out the window, she kept fondling the soft edges of her beloved scarf.

"Rosie," Hope said softly, "someone wants to talk to you."

Ms. Anders pushed through the door and entered the room.

Rosie turned to see the social worker. The stiffness of the woman frightened her. She shrank back and turned to face the window.

"Thank you, Ms. Abrams. Close the door on your way out."

Rosie hurried to hide behind Hope. "I want Hope to stay..."

"She'll be downstairs." The lady's voice sounded stern.

"I'm sorry, baby," Hope squeezed her around the waist, "but I'm not allowed to stay. Be brave."

After close to forty-five minutes, Ms. Anders came

downstairs with Rosie following behind, holding the now-stuffed leather bag. With a downcast face, the girl avoided eye contact with the two anxious women who sat in jitters on the couch.

"Rose and I had a good little chat, didn't we?" She glared at the girl until she forced a nod. "Rose has agreed to come with me, and she understands why."

"But...why can't she stay here?" Hope asked.

"You've harbored a runaway, and we will deal with that later. For now, Rose must be placed where we know she is safe."

"But she's safe here—" Hope began.

Ms. Anders gave her a stern look.

"It's okay," Rosie swiped at the tear running down her cheek. Swallowing the lump in her throat, Rosie slowly shuffled to Ms. Anders' car. Before getting in the backseat, she dared to peek at the pitiful ladies standing in the doorway. Tears were in their eyes, too. She held tightly to the leather bag and let herself cry.

"Please," she pleaded to the lady in the driver's seat. "Don't send Hope and Faith to jail. I was good and came with you. I did everything you wanted me to do. I even told you my last name, so please–please leave them alone."

"They did wrong, Rose. They kept you there without telling anyone."

"No! No! They only helped me. They were good to

me." She banged the back of the seat with her feet.

"Calm down, young lady, or you'll be sorry." The social worker took an icy tone. "Remember what I told you. You don't want to make me mad...."

Rosie had heard those words before. It struck a new fear in her soul. She clamped her mouth closed, remembering how Nina punished her whenever she made the woman mad. *I won't tell this woman anything,* Rosie promised herself.

11 - SEARCH FOR ANSWERS

Ms. Anders showed Rosie into a waiting area with a couch, a few chairs, and a television. "Someone will be here to get you right away," Ms. Anders said. "I'll only be a minute and check back to see how you're doing."

All alone, Rosie shivered more from fear than from cold. She surveyed the musty-smelling room. Old board games and puzzles without pieces sat on the end table. Pictures saying "Believe" and "Dream" gave her little hope as they hung crooked on the wall.

Hugging tightly to the leather bag, she tried to watch television but couldn't help but worry about the trouble she may have caused for Faith and Hope. *Help them be okay, God. It's the only reason I came with this lady.*

Ms. Anders notified the supervisor of Rosie's arrival and went to her office. She clicked on her laptop and pulled up the state database for missing children. Nothing. She put it into the national database. Again, nothing. Plenty of missing twelve-year-old girls, but none named Delahunt. And none from anywhere around the Ridgetown area. Picking up her phone, she called the doctor who notified CPS of the girl.

"Dr. Edwards? This is Stacey Anders, Child Protective Services. I'm calling about the twelve-year-old girl with a crooked leg and a scar on her face."

"Yes?" replied the doctor.

"The girl's full name is Rose Delahunt. She lived in Abbotsville. I thought it might be helpful in your search for medical information."

"Yes. Yes, the last name will be a tremendous help," agreed the doctor. "I've already researched all files going back ten years for anyone with the name Rose or Rosie without success. Having a location and last name will help narrow the search. Thank you."

"Oh, and Doctor? Have you checked the birth records? We need to know her mother's and father's names. I'm pulling blanks here."

"Already working on it. I'll keep you posted."

Hanging up the phone, the doctor clicked on his laptop and opened birth records for the surrounding counties. He typed in the last name and pulled up birth records for twelve years earlier. Within seconds, he found a record for the birth of Rosalita Rae Delahunt. The mother's name was listed as Carmen Rae Delahunt; the father's name was unknown. The address on the record read: 223 Bradey Court, Abbotsville, Missouri. He called back the social worker within the hour.

"This is good news, Doctor." Ms. Anders scribbled the address on a notepad. "I will drive to Abbotsville myself and check this address. Let's hope someone's there. Thank you for your help."

Across town, the sisters were distraught. "Why do you suppose Rosie went so willingly with Ms. Anders?" Faith questioned, dabbing moisture from her eyes. "I miss her already."

"I don't know, but it worries me to death," said Hope, "you saw the fear and uncertainty in her face. She couldn't even look at us."

"We'll pray, sister," said Faith. "Pray for God's best and for His protection around Rosie."

Hope picked up her cell phone. "I'm going to call Pastor Jim. I just don't know what else to do." Explaining the situation to her minister brought her to tears. "What should we do?"

"Well, Hope, there's nothing much more you can do besides pray. Rosie is now in the hands of the social services."

"What happens in the meantime?"

"They will keep her until they find more information. Then they will look for someone who knows her."

"Oh, I just wish she could stay with us while they investigate. At least then we know she'd be safe and warm, happy and fed."

"I know you do, Hope. Sadly, that's not how it works."

"What if they don't find anyone?"

"She'll go into foster care until they find a relative. If they find no one, she may end up for adoption."

"Pastor...." Hope broached the subject, "aren't you and Mary certified as foster parents?"

Hope's question stopped him short. "Hmmm...yes, we are certified and licensed by the State of Missouri. But we mostly take in little children under the age of five as temporary assignments. Why do you ask?"

"Well..." she paused until he wondered if she'd hung up, "maybe God's opening the door for you to take in an older child?"

The preacher cleared his throat, caught off guard with Hope's persistence.

Rosie fidgeted on the couch twisting her curls around her fingers. *Where is she?* She dug through the stuffed leather bag, checking to make sure all her clothes and especially her gold scarf was there. Certain everything was accounted for, she sorted through the few pieces of the jigsaw puzzle on the end table.

Ms. Anders found Rosie studying the puzzle. "Sorry I had to leave you alone, Rose. I thought the supervisor was coming immediately to take you to your cubicle."

I have to stay here? Overnight?

Now her stomach really did hurt.

12 - WHAT NOW?

"I have to go home now," Ms. Anders said, "but I'll be back in the morning. Someone should come soon."

The lady supervisor came through the door just as Ms. Anders was leaving. "Rose? Rose Delahunt?"

Why did I have to tell my last name? She tricked me, that's why. Rosie moaned and arose from the couch.

"Busy day. Sorry it took so long. Looks like you'll be staying with us a while. Hurry along now and come with me." Barely waiting long enough for Rosie to get off the couch, she turned and began to walk away.

Rosie grabbed the bag and hurried to follow the lady with the frazzled look who sounded like she'd already had a hard day.

"This side of the building is for the girls," she told Rosie. "The other side is where the boys stay."

A row of cubicles with half walls and no doors lined the interior hallway. They passed one cubicle where a small girl sat on her cot reading a comic book. The next cubicle held a girl in her mid-teens, looking at a fashion magazine. She glanced up at Rosie with an unimpressed look. The supervisor pointed to the cubicle next to her.

"The girl who had this space left yesterday. So, now it's your sleeping quarters. Dinner is in one-half hour. Breakfast at 7:00 a.m. Don't be late. The girls' shower room is down the hall to the right. You may want to get there early." With that, she turned and left.

Rosie sat down on the hard cot and put her head in her hands. 'Hold on to faith' she heard Hope's words replay in her mind. 'Don't give up hope... be brave.' Overwhelmed, she began to sob. Gut-wrenching gulps of air escaped with each breath. *What have I done wrong? What will I do now?*

"What's wrong with you?" came a voice from the next cubicle. The older girl peered around the corner.

Rosie's body trembled as she held in the sobs. Drawing her legs up to her chest, she buried her head between her knees and tried to stifle her sobs. "I'm scared."

Julie came around and sat down cross-legged beside Rosie. "First time?"

Rosie caught her voice in her throat. "Ye...ah."

"Well, ya better get used to it. You may be here a while, maybe weeks."

Rosie looked up with wrinkles of worry. "Weeks?"

"Guessing you ran away."

Rosie's eyes got large. She opened her mouth in surprise, but nothing came out. She shook her head in confusion. "But I didn't... uh... run away."

"Yeah, sure. I bet you have some fancy-dancy parents coming to get you right away, too." Julie flipped her head.

Rosie felt like she would break into tears again. Swallowing hard, she could only shake her head.

"Just sayin'.... Don't try to run away from here. They'll find you every time. Believe me, I know." Julie grew quiet as she reflected upon her own past. "Guys out there will promise you all kinds of things—" she went on. "Pretty clothes, jewelry... say they even love you, but they lie. They *all* lie." Her voice took on a pang of sadness and too much bitterness for one so young. She sighed. "Sometimes... they hurt you... sometimes... they won't let you leave...."

Rosie stared at Julie as she spoke, her heart beating faster. She hugged her knees even closer to her body.

"Yeah," Julie continued, squeezing her eyes tight as if to shut out the memory. "If I wouldn't have escaped from Dex, I'd probably be dead–or worse," she paused to bite her nails that were already bitten to the quick.

Or worse? What could be worse than dead?

"It was lucky for me that I ran when Dex was drunk. I waited until he passed out and then ran as fast as I could to the only safe place I could think of. I came back here because, well, because I couldn't go home. Been eight months now."

"Eight *months*?" Rosie whispered.

"Things take time – especially when you're my age. So, like I said, get used to it but watch your stuff." She pointed to the cubicle on the other side, "Maddie is a klepto."

"Klepto?" Rosie repeated with a frown shaking her head.

"Klep-to-man-i-ac," Julie pronounced each syllable slowly. "She likes to steal."

"Oh." Rosie sighed.

"By the way, I'm Julie. What's your name?" She stood up to go back to her cot.

"Rosie." It came out like a squeak.

The girl from the next cubicle poked her little head over the half wall and watched as Rosie pulled her belongings from the bag. "Hi, Rosie," she giggled with an impish grin. "I'm Maddie. Hey, what's wrong with your face?"

"Wondered that myself. Fall when you ran with scissors?" Julie hooted.

Rosie's face crinkled.

"I'm joking. Come on, you thought it was funny."

"No, it wasn't. It was mean." Rosie put her hand quickly over her cheek. "It's...the dev—uh, it's nothing," stammered Rosie.

"Okay. Whatever. You'll fit in good around here."

What's that mean? Rosie felt that unwanted lump in her throat coming up again.

"Ya ready to go eat, Scarey Face?" teased Maddie.

"Aw, leave her alone," scolded Julie. "She's gonna cry again."

Rosie swallowed hard, pushed the last of her clothes in the drawer, and painfully pulled herself up. "Yeah. I'm ready."

Ms. Anders was glad for an address to work with. Punching the address into her GPS, she navigated the ten miles to the little berg of Abbotsville, southwest of Ridgetown.

She knocked. No answer. Peering into a window, all she could see was darkness inside. The lawn hadn't been mowed for a couple of weeks and the rose garden was full of weeds.

A younger woman was working outside her house in the yard next door. "Can I help you?"

Ms. Anders walked over, introduced herself, and then asked about the neighbors.

"Sorry. I only moved here a few months ago. A woman lived there with a young girl, but I didn't know them. Saw them come and go. I'm not too neighborly, but neither were they."

Discouraged at the lack of help, Ms. Anders

thanked her, got into her car and left. It was time to call in some help.

13 - IN HOLDING

“C’mon. Let’s go eat. Can’t be late.”

Rosie twisted her long hair around her fingers as she followed Julie to the dining hall making sure it hid her scar.

“You walk funny,” Maddie pestered from behind.

Rosie turned around, tightened her lips into a pucker and crossed her eyes at Maddie.

“Well, you do,” Maddie said.

“I’ve got a dumb leg. Okay? I can’t help it.”

“Limpy. Wimpy,” Maddie sang a little tune.

Julie laughed. “Boy, you really will fit in good with all us misfits.”

Rosie’s heart sank.

The dining room held several long cafeteria tables, enough to fit twenty people. The girls picked up their food cafeteria style and lifted their legs over the bench. Rosie tried a couple of times, but her bad leg would not lift that high.

“You really are lame, aren’t ya?” said Julie with a sneer. “Here. Scoot in from the end.”

In between bites, Rosie saw close to a dozen boys

and girls of different ages.

"Maddie's been here several times. Ain't that right, little girl?" Julie poked the young girl's arm.

"Um-hmm. Daddy's in prison and Mama keeps getting into trouble. The police came got her again last week. They brought me here. In and out. Every time, Mama goes back to jail." Maddie acted as if she didn't care as she slurped her glass of milk.

"Oh." Rosie took a small bite of her PB&J sandwich.

"I hope to get good foster parents this time, and don't have to share a bed with other kids," Maddie chattered on.

"Other kids?" Rosie's stomach fluttered.

"Yeah. Sure. Sometimes there's bunches of other kids."

The flutters began to tie themselves into knots. Rosie took a drink hoping to settle the discomfort.

"I've been lots of places. One time, it was just me and I really liked them. They liked me too. I wanted them to adopt me, but they were too old. Besides CPS always makes me go back to live with Mama."

"What's CPS?"

"Child Protective Services. They're supposed to 'protect' us," Julie emphasized. "Sometimes, we wonder."

"Oh." Rosie's thoughts felt jumbled. Her

stomachache was getting worse.

"What's your story?" asked Julie.

I don't dare say anything. She was feeling sicker by the moment. "Uh...Ms. Anders showed up and then brought me here. I hope I don't have to stay long...." Her voice trailed off.

"Got somewhere to go?" laughed Julie as she finished the last bite.

Rosie shook her head, not hungry anymore. "No. There's no one." *—except for Hope and Faith and they sure won't let me go back there.*

About an hour before lights out, Rosie whispered over the wall. "Julie, Will you go with me to the restroom? I'm scared."

"Come on, you're a big girl. You don't need me. Or are ya a baby? Ya gonna cry again? Bathroom's at the end of the hall. Take your PJs and shower tonight, if you're smart."

"Why?"

"You'll see."

Rosie dug out her pajamas, sucked in her breath, and snuck down the long, darkened hall alone. Every time the dimmed lights flickered. It made her flinch. The shadows danced like goblins ready to pounce at any moment. About to forget the shower, she almost turned around when she found the door.

I'm here now. I can do this. The squeaky bathroom

door made her heart race. She hurriedly flipped on the light and jumped backwards as cockroaches scurried everywhere. *I can do this....*

The shower rooms were to the right of the toilet area. Rosie's mouth dropped open. Now she knew why the supervisor said to come early. No doors, no privacy. Never having been to a public school gym, this was all new to her.

Be brave, Rosie, she told herself.

Slipping out of her clothes, Rosie stepped under the running water. She lifted her head up to wash her hair and saw cobwebs lining the corners of the ceiling. Her breathing became shallow as her imagination went wild with gigantic spiders. She hurried to finish, wanting to get out of this place. *What could be worse?*

Stacey Anders had decided it was time to call in more help. She googled local detectives and came upon the name of John Flanders, a private detective from around Queen City. His credentials looked superior. She took a chance and tapped in the number.

"Detective John Flanders."

"Good day, Detective," said Stacey Anders. After exchanging pleasantries, she explained the reason for her call. "We may have a runaway girl, but we're not sure. We suspect there may have been physical abuse."

"I see. Quite distinguishing marks," commented

the Detective after hearing the description of the girl. "What's she telling you?"

"Not much. Have there been any police reports of missing children around here?"

"No, there haven't, and that's a bit strange if she ran away. What's her name?"

"Her name is Rose Delahunt. Said she lived with someone she called Nina over in Abbotsville."

"Down toward the Branson area. Who's Nina?"

"No idea. That's why I'm calling you. I drove there yesterday hoping to find her or Carmen. With your credentials, you can dig deeper. Search the house. Find out if Carmen is around and who Nina is. You, know, snoop for clues."

"Carmen's the mother?"

"According to the birth certificate."

"Well, it's something to start on. Delahunt, you say? Abbotsville?"

"Yes. Do you want the case?"

"I'll get on it, A.S.A.P."

"Thank you, Detective. We need to find out what really happened so we can get this girl back home. I hope my suspicion of abuse is wrong."

14 - THE REPORT

"Ms. Anders called today," said Faith as she pulled a tray of cookies from the oven.

"Who?"

"The lady from Social Services who took Rosie."

Hope scrunched her nose in disgust. "Oh. What did she want?"

"She wants to talk to us–something about a follow-up report. She's coming this afternoon. Figured I'd bake some cookies to encourage her to be more friendly."

"But we told her everything we know." Hope swiped a hot cookie off the counter. "Mmmm. Good, sis."

"Maybe she found something more to tell us?"

"She wouldn't tell us anything. I only hope we're not in trouble."

Ms. Anders knocked on the Abrams sisters' door at the appointed time. Faith showed her the way to the kitchen. "We fixed refreshments, Ms. Anders. Please, make yourself comfortable."

The caseworker lifted her nose and sniffed the aroma of warm coconut cookies. It brought a smile to her face. "Thank you. This visit is a matter of formality, that's all. Normally if we suspect child abuse, we must follow up with a written report."

Faith's eyes widened as she set the plate of cookies on the table, poured iced tea, and then sat down. "Child abuse? Our Rosie wasn't— We didn't abuse her, ma'am."

Ms. Anders took a sip of sweet tea and helped herself to a cookie. "I'm not implying you did. From what Dr. Edwards reported, he suspected abuse. Not only physically, but emotionally and psycho-logically. There are telltale signs."

"We really don't know any more than what we told you the first time. We found her and brought her here. We fed her, let her bathe, and gave her a bed to sleep in," Faith said.

Hope spoke up. "We gave the girl compassion. We showed her God's love."

"I understand, ladies." Ms. Anders held both hands up for them to stop speaking. "By the way, these cookies are delicious. I love coconut." She took another bite and then washed it down with tea.

"Our mother's recipe," said Faith with a smile. "Coconut macaroons."

"I'd love the recipe for these." She finished the cookie and grabbed another. "I have no doubt your compassion was real and innocent. It's the only reason

I won't press charges against you."

"Charges? What kind of charges?" Hope was aghast.

"The law mandates you call the authorities and report a runaway or child abuse within twenty-four hours of learning about it. You did not do this."

"Sorry. We didn't know—" They gulped and looked at each other in dismay. Faith began to twist her necklace.

Ms. Ander took another sip of tea and wiped her mouth with the napkin. "Did you know the penalty for failing to report any case to the police, to a doctor, or to a social worker can be up to six months in jail, or at the least $1,000 fine? Sometimes both." Ms. Anders raised her voice to emphasize the seriousness of the matter.

Faith choked on a piece of cookie. "Mercy me!" She gave Hope a 'what-do-we-do-now' look. "We just tried to help her and thought we were doing what was best."

"I understand." Ms. Anders softened her voice. "Don't worry. I'm not here to accuse you or have you arrested. You ladies may have answers about Rosie you don't even realize. I have an investigator checking to find if she ran away or escaped from someplace. We must find out *why* she left. At this time, we don't believe she was lost or kidnapped."

"That's what we came to believe, too."

Ms. Anders pulled her cellphone from her purse. "Do you mind if I record our conversation? It will help me transcribe the report easier." She laid her phone on the table to pick up their voices. "As I said before, there are telltale signs for abuse. For instance, the day I came to talk to Rose, she cowered in the corner of her room stroking a gold scarf. That told me she was clearly anxious and afraid."

"Yes, she was very fearful the day I found her. She reared back from me when I first tried to help her up from the ditch," said Hope. "I finally convinced her to come with me."

"Reared back as if you would strike her?"

"Why, yes. And she didn't talk for at least four days. We thought she might be mute."

Ms. Anders nodded. "What else?"

"She pulled her knees up to her chest whenever we pried too much for answers. It usually followed with total silence and blank stares," added Faith.

"...or a stomachache," remembered Hope. "She often said her tummy hurt."

"All signs of emotional abuse," said the caseworker. "Did she go out of her way to please you?"

Faith stared at the table and drew circles with her finger. "Why, yes, she did. We thought she was just getting more comfortable with us. She did anything we asked of her."

"Um-hmm. She didn't want to make you mad or upset," Ms. Anders reasoned.

"Poor girl. Remember, Faith? I told you from day one Rosie was hurt by someone or something deep within her soul. I could sense it the way she clung to me."

"And you ladies offered her a safe haven without judgment."

"Of course we did," Hope put her hands on her large hips. "It was the *right thing* to do."

"And we praised her whenever we could," added Faith.

Ms. Anders nodded with approval. "Did you see any bruises?" asked the social worker.

"She had scrapes and cuts. I figured it was from falling. She bathed and dressed on her own, so if she had others anywhere else, we wouldn't have known."

"The only visible thing we saw was her scar and her limp."

"How is our Rosie doing?" Hope asked. "We miss her so much. She was only here a week, but she brought new life into this old house."

"She's adapting."

"Have you found her parents yet?" Faith asked as she refilled the glasses.

"Still working on it, but Rose is a mystery. Sorry. I can't give you any more details of an ongoing investigation."

"When she does get placed somewhere," asked Hope, "will we be allowed to visit her?" Hope offered the lady another cookie.

The caseworker scowled. "That's not advisable, ladies. The child must acclimate to new surroundings. We will also try to get her back to where she belongs as soon as possible."

Hope's face dropped. "Well, I'm going to pray for a way to make it happen. God can make a way when all seems hopeless."

Ms. Anders raised an eyebrow but said nothing. She clicked the recorder off and rose from the table. "You've both been very helpful. I have enough for a complete report now. Thank you for the cookies and tea."

"Can you tell Rosie hello for us? Tell her we're praying for her?" asked Hope.

"No promises," said the woman as they walked her to the door. "Good day, ladies."

15 – ABBOTSVILLE

Detective Flanders put the address into his GPS and navigated to the western outskirts of the town, and then south toward Bradey Road. He parked on the curb beside the mailbox that had 'Delahunt' stenciled it. The cottage was locked tight, as Ms. Anders indicated. As he walked to the house next door, he saw an older woman sitting on her porch watching him from the opposite side of the street. Acknowledging her with a nod, he knocked on the next-door neighbor's door. She told him about her conversation with the social worker and then referred him to 'Mrs. Know-it-all' across the street.

Her answer placed a smile on the detective's lips. "Who?"

"Mrs. Walters." The lady waved to the older woman. "She's the gossip in the neighborhood. Knows everybody's business. She was at my door with nut bread the day I moved in wanting to know everything about me."

The detective thanked her and walked across the street to an older A-framed cottage surrounded by hydrangeas. The older woman sat in her white wicker rocker crocheting from the ball of yarn in her lap.

"Mrs. Walters?"

An abundance of happy wrinkles creased her forehead. She set her crochet hook down and pushed her glasses up higher on her nose as she smiled to look up at him. "Call me Hazel. What can I do for you, young man?"

The detective smiled at the compliment. "I'm looking for Ms. Delahunt." He pointed across the street.

"Ohhh, I see. Another gentleman caller, are you?" She reached up to tap his ring finger. She clucked her tongue. "And a married man at that. My, my, my."

She reminded him of his own grandmother who might scold him for a misdeed. It made him blush and laugh out loud. "Oh! No! Nothing like that. I'm John Flanders from Queen City Investigative Services."

Her tone switched from rebuke to curiosity. "Then what's all this about, detective?"

"The child who lived with her...."

"You mean Rosie?" She cut in.

"Yes, Rosie." He arched his eyebrows. "She was found near Ridgetown—"

"Oh, my," Hazel gasped. "Is she all right?"

"Yes, she's fine, ma'am. She is in protective custody right now with Child Protective Services. I'm trying to locate Ms. Delahunt to find out what's going on. May I ask you a few questions?"

"Oh my, yes!" She set her crochet hook and yarn in the nearby basket and rose slowly from her rocker. "Please, come in. It will be delightful to talk to such a nice good-looking young man like you." Slipping her arm through his, she guided him into the kitchen, patting his arm. "I'll put on the coffee pot."

Detective Flanders took a seat at the table and removed his notebook and pen from his coat pocket. "Thank you, Mrs. Walters. Please, tell me what you know."

"Hazel, please, dear."

Over coffee, Hazel Walters related how the Delahunt's moved into the neighborhood over twelve years before. "I've lived here for over twenty years and nothing escapes these peepers." She tapped her glasses. "I've seen neighbors come and go and learned every one of their stories."

"I'm sure you have, Mrs. Walters." The detective looked at his watch and tapped his pen on the pad, trying his best to be sociable.

"Call me Hazel, dear. I try to be a good neighbor to everyone." Hazel's brown eyes twinkled. "So, I took her some nut bread and my welcoming disposition."

"You were a good friend to her then?"

"Of course. I tried to get her to tell me all about herself, but she didn't chatter too much about her past.

I can see everything going on over there though, mind you."

"Have you noticed anything strange lately?"

She puckered her lips in thought. "It's been a few weeks, but yes, maybe I have."

"What's that?"

"It may be my imagination, but I swear I've noticed a light coming from the attic window." She cupped her hand to her mouth in a whisper. "And you know those little cottages don't have much of an upstairs."

"Where?"

She moseyed over to the front window holding her hip as she did. Pulling back the drapes, she pointed. "See that tiny window? Up in the top area of that cottage? It's crusted over with grime, but every now and then – until it stopped a few weeks ago – I swore there was a glimmer of light trying to poke through–like someone trying to peer out, or get my attention, or something."

"Are you saying Rosie's bedroom was in the attic?"

"Oh, I'm not saying anything of the sort, Detective. I only thought it was curious, that's all. After all," she gave him a sly wink, "you're the detective. It made me wonder whether the girl was trying to signal me for help or something–if you know what I mean." She ambled back to the kitchen, poured them more coffee and eased her aching hip back onto her chair.

"I'll check it out, ma'am." Detective Flanders followed and sat.

"Call me Hazel, dear."

"Yes, ma'am. I'll look into it." He rose to leave and then asked, "Mrs. Walters, have you seen them recently–like within the last couple of weeks?"

She pursed her lips. "Please. Call me Hazel." She thought a few minutes as her ruffled feathers smoothed. "No, can't say as I have. Figured they were probably on vacation or something. Now, mind you, I'm not one who noses in on other people's business, but I've seen an awful lot of men come and go from that house–if you know what I mean." She winked again.

The detective nodded and jotted a note. Her imagination made him grin.

"If you want my humble opinion, sir...."

"As if I had a choice," he muttered under his breath.

"I began to think Carmen was like her mom."

"Meaning?"

"Oh, posh," Hazel said. "Forgive me. That was very judgmental of me. Nothing, Sir."

The detective jotted a few more notes to follow up on. "One last question, Mrs. Walters..."

She gave him a glare.

"Hazel. Sorry." He grinned. "Did Ms. Delahunt

own her home, or did she rent? Do you know?"

"Well, that I know for a fact. She had a man who paid the rent. She didn't have to worry about that. No, siree. She paid him in other ways." She wagged her head. "If you know what I mean."

"Know his name?"

"Benny, I think. Benny something."

Flanders scratched a few more notes and rose to leave. "Thank you, Hazel. You've been very helpful today."

"Next time you come, I'll have a chocolate cake ready," she smiled sweetly.

Driving back toward Ridgetown, Detective Flanders' felt good about the trip, but now there were also more questions than answers. If he could get into Delahunt's house and search further, he might find out more about Carmen Delahunt and her daughter, Rosie. But first, he'd have to find the landlord for a key.

16 - HOUSE SEARCH

John Flanders headed directly to the county public offices. The Records Office would give him owner information and land titles.

"May I have the plat maps and land titles for Abbotsville?" he asked the clerk.

Finding a seat in the conference room, he followed the list of addresses with his finger until landing upon 223 Bradey Court. He wrote down the name and telephone number of the owner and returned the ledger to the desk. Back in his car, he tapped in the number and fidgeted in his seat while the phone continued to ring on the other end. Maybe this would lead to some better answers. Finally, someone answered.

"Mr. Barnes? Detective John Flanders." The detective told him what he needed and then asked for a key to search the house on Brady Court.

"Whatcha lookin' for, Detective?"

"Anything to help me track down Carmen Delahunt."

Barnes coughed. "Ah... is there... trouble?"

"Police matters, sir. I can't give you details. You

understand."

"Ah, sure. Um.... anything to do with... uh... the girl?" The man's raspy cough caught in his throat.

This time it was Detective Flanders' turn to choke back a response. "Again," uh... under investigation. I just need to look around. What's the best time to meet you there?"

"Well... uh... let's see," Mr. Barnes's voice raised higher. "How 'bout 2:00 p.m. tomorrow? Better have a search warrant."

"Works for me. And don't worry, I'll have the warrant ready."

As soon as he ended the call with Flanders, Rusty received a call from Benny. His shrill voice unnerved her. "Rusty! A cop's asking about you. Wantin' to search the house. Whadja do wrong?" The panic in his voice was evident.

"Just living and working at your place, Benny, is criminal enough. You didn't tell him I'm with you, did you?"

"I'm not stupid, woman. He doesn't even know who I am, and I don't intend to give him a hint."

A shudder went through Rusty's body. She'd felt uneasy ever since coming back to Benny. He'd given her a room upstairs like so many years before–the same room where she had raised her own daughter,

Carmen. Benny seemed glad to have her back. Said she was good for business. Said she'd filled the empty spot in his life. And the best part? She didn't have to raise a crippled kid.

Flanders waited in his car by the curb outside the Delahunt house one-half hour early with a search warrant in hand. He saw Hazel Walters peering out her window. He waved; she waved back. *She doesn't miss a thing.*

Mr. Barnes pulled up exactly at 2:00 p.m. The stocky man with a bulging stomach got out of his truck. Flanders shook the man's rough hand as they exchanged greetings. Mr. Barnes unlocked the front door and had to duck to let his almost six-foot body through the entrance.

The detective ran his finger along the shelf raising the dust as he did. "Looks like no one's been here for a while."

"Can I help ya look for sumpthin'?" Mr. Barnes rubbed his bulbous nose.

"Thanks, but I prefer to look alone. You can come back in an hour or so."

"Nah, I'll wait." He kicked at dust bunnies on the floor.

Flanders shrugged. "Up to you." He headed toward the kitchen off the front room.

Barnes plopped uneasily on the couch and straightened an untidy stack of magazines and stuffed a few papers underneath them on the coffee table. He lit a cigarette, picked up a magazine and began to leaf uneasily through the pages.

The kitchen was small but efficient. A couple of unwashed pans still sat in the sink. A wrap-around booth covered with vinyl seats filled the corner. Finding nothing noteworthy, Flanders wandered through the living room. Mr. Barnes pushed the butt of his cigarette in the ashtray, warily eyeing the detective as he passed.

Flanders entered a side bedroom. *Probably Rosie's*. It was small with only a single bed and dresser. The opened dresser drawers were empty. A rag rug covered the bare cracked linoleum floor by the bed. Turning his flashlight to the inside of the closet, he noticed markings on the wall. Not sure what they signified, he took some pictures with his phone.

The main bedroom was next. The bed was unmade, clothes were strewn about the floor.

"Whatcha looking for?" Mr. Barnes asked again poking his nose into the bedroom.

"A clue, Barnes. Any clue to find the whereabouts of the mother of the child," he baited.

"You mean Carmen?"

"Yes. What do you know about her?"

Mr. Barnes shifted his weight from foot to foot and stuffed his large hands in his pockets. "Uuuh..." he stammered. "N-n-nuthin', really."

Flanders bit the inside of his cheek. "Almost finished. I need to check the attic."

A very narrow stairway led the way to an upper storage room. Unable to stand up straight, he ducked under the sloped slats of the ceiling. A few old boxes scattered here and there. Shattered glass lay on the floor but no evidence of blood. In the back, an old chest of drawers stood warped and cracked with several faded pictures laying on top. He picked up a photo showing a young mother holding a toddler. *Evidence of happier days. Carmen and Rosie*–and then looking more closely, he scribbled a note: *Baby in picture has red curly hair like her mother's. Rosie has black hair.* Snapped more pictures.

The opened trunk in the back held several old blouses, jeans, pants, dresses, sweaters–all teen sizes. Packed away and forgotten. *Rosie's clothes? But why would they smell musty? Something doesn't feel right here.*

Waving his flashlight at a rubbed-out patch of dirt on the window he saw Mrs. Walters had moved outside to her chair on the front porch. It caught her eye. He grinned when he remembered her worries. She didn't miss a thing, but there was no bedroom up here.

He came back downstairs and found Barnes puffing on his third cigarette. Out of the corner of his eye, he noticed a matchbook laying on the coffee table. He could make out three letters from where he stood: B-E-N.

"Find anything?" Barnes fidgeted.

"Maybe."

As Barnes got up from the couch, John Flanders swiped the matchbook without being seen and stuffed it into his pocket. "Just one more question. Did Carmen pay the rent here or someone else?"

"Ummm...." Barnes scratched his balding head and frowned as if trying to think. "Maybe." He pulled his pants up and inhaled deeply. "As long as the bills got paid, it's of no matter to me."

"Surely you must know. Have a name? Who paid the rent?"

"I'd...uh...well...have to look it up...back at the office."

Struck a nerve. "I heard a man named Benny helped out. Is he the one who paid the rent?"

Barnes's face flushed. Beads of sweat ran down his forehead. His eyes were big and round, but he kept his composure. "I-I-I'll...uh...check the books." He cleared his throat and coughed. "'Scuse me. I need a drink." The man hurried toward the kitchen as Flanders took one more look around.

Once in his car, he pulled the matchbook from his pocket. The front had the inscription: *Benny's Place*. He flipped it over in his hand and felt as if he'd found gold.

Detective Flanders hadn't uncovered much, but he was happy to find the matchbook with an address. Arriving at his Queen City office, he immediately called CPS to inform Ms. Anders of his findings. He was forwarded to Anders' out-of-office message. He left a voice mail in shortened clips.

"Ms. Anders. You were correct. Carmen left fast. Found strange markings in the closet. Call me."

When the social worker called the detective back, Flanders relayed his findings.

"You mentioned there were strange markings in the closet. What did they look like?" she asked.

"Just scribblings on the lower parts of the wall with a crayon, that's all."

"Hmmm...." The caseworker's intuition kicked in. "By the way, I have news for you too. You were searching for a dead woman."

"What do you mean?"

"Carmen hasn't lived at the Abbotsville home for over ten years. Dr. Edwards found a death certificate. She died a few months after the accident."

"Ugh. Barnes led me to believe Carmen was alive." He sniffed. "Why? I may have to make another visit to

'Mrs. Know-it-all'."

"Excuse me?"

"Delahunt's neighbor. I think she knew all along Carmen wasn't alive. I may get a few more answers from her if I sweet-talk her."

Back at the brothel, Benny was having a panic attack. His breath came in short gasps as he poured himself another drink with a shaky hand.

"Benny! What's wrong with you? Looks like you've seen a ghost," Rusty brushed her hand across his stubbled cheek.

"Rusty, I didn't tell that man anything. I swear. He searched all through your house; I stayed there and watched. Don't think he found nuthin'. Still thinks Carmen lives there, not you."

"You're sure you didn't tip him off?" Rusty asked.

"No, woman," he answered, sounding indignant that she would ask. "Said he's trying to find the kid's mother."

Rusty felt a tremble go through her body. "What did you tell him?"

"Nuthin', Rus'–nuthing'. Honest."

17 - THE MISSING SCARF

Awakening in the holding area the next morning, Rosie's body ached from the hard cot; her skin itched from the scratchy blankets. She had tossed and turned all night thinking about Hope and Faith. She was just as tired as when she went to bed. The girls on either side of her began to rise.

"Get up, Limpy," Maddie rapped on the wall. "Shower time!"

Rosie slowly sat up and rubbed her leg. "Already been there," she called back, glad she'd showered the night before. "See you at breakfast, Maddie."

As she picked out clothes for the day, her heart sank. *Where is it? My gold scarf. It's gone! The only thing I have of my mother's. I know I put it in here last night.* Fear. Anger. Bewilderment. All emotions rushed to the surface at once. She dug with fierceness through the dresser drawer, pulling out every item. Close to tears, she reached behind the drawer, looked underneath the cot and dresser. Then she remembered Maddie sneaking peeks over the wall when she put her things away.

Klepto. Watch your things. Julie warned her.

Maddie!

Fuming all the way to the dining hall, Rosie tried to think how to accuse Maddie. She didn't have to wonder long. There sat Maddie in all her eight-year-old glory with a smug grin on her face–and Rosie's gold scarf draped around her neck.

Rosie gritted her teeth and stomped over to the little girl. She pointed to the scarf. "How dare you. That's my scarf!" she shouted.

"Whaaat?" Maddie flicked the scarf over her shoulder and tossed her blond hair. "I found it in the TV room on the floor. Now, it's mine." She stuck her nose in the air and smirked. "Finders Keepers. Losers Weepers."

"No, you didn't! It was in my drawer! MY space. MY scarf." Rosie burned a hole into Maddie with her eyes. She yanked at the scarf on Maddie's neck and pulled with all her might. Maddie fell off the chair to the floor leaving Rosie grasping the scarf to her chest.

"OW!" Maddie wailed, curling herself into a little ball. "I found it. I swear."

"Liar." Rosie gave Maddie a kick.

"Break it up, girls." The dining hall monitor rushed toward the commotion to pull them apart. "What's this all about?"

"My scarf! She took it." Rosie accused, pointing at Maddie who lay crying on the floor.

"It looks like it's in your hands now, miss."

Angry, Rosie clutched the beloved scarf close to her heart and stomped back to her cubicle. She wasn't hungry anymore. This scarf–her mother's scarf–was part of the reason Nina kicked her out. She couldn't afford to lose it now.

She sat on the edge of the cot and gathered the wrap together in a ball. Holding it to her face, she sniffed in the sweet perfume and recalled the time Nina first found her with this sacred covering. The tormented memories made her shudder....

All the way home from the beach, Rosie had stifled the sobs that wanted to spill out. *Nina's so mad. Why? Why does Nina hate me so much? I don't understand.*

Once they arrived back home, she escaped to her forbidden sanctuary in the attic, knowing Nina was mad enough to leave her alone for a while. She sat beside the dirt-encrusted window and pulled the gold scarf from its secret hiding place. It caught a few rays of sunlight and glimmered. *It always looks so new.* Its softness made her feel safe. She stroked the satin ribbon woven through the edges, held the wrap close to her face, and wept.

When she looked up, she caught a glimpse of herself in the cracked mirror. *Look! The curse is gone! The scarf covers my awful mark.* She smiled at her reflection. *I have a magic scarf to take me anywhere I want to go–far away from here.*

Rosie's imagination carried her away to a fantasy world far from harm and hurt. She draped it over her head, tossed one side over her shoulder, and pretended to be a Spanish senorita. Next, she was a princess escaping on her white horse with her veil flowing in the wind. Bowing in front of the mirror, she imagined herself a young bride glowing behind the silken veil in the soft candlelight of a wedding chapel.

Maybe a dancer. Rosie flung the scarf into the air. *I wish I could dance!* She dreamed of being a ballerina. She threw her arms into the air in a ballet pose and attempted to stand on her tiptoes and twirl. Losing her balance as the ankle of her crooked foot turned, she tripped on a box. In pain, she grabbed a lamp stand to help break her fall. It tumbled over, crashing her into boxes and tins as she landed into a crumpled heap on the floor. Rosie cringed. *Oh no! Nina had to have heard the crash.* Before she could gather her wits and get downstairs, she heard Nina running up the steps.

"You stupid oaf!" Nina's face was crimson. Darts of hate through Nina's narrowed eyes pierced Rosie's heart.

"Sorry," Rosie whimpered, her head hung low.

"You were WARNED," Nina screamed shaking her finger at her. "This place is FORBIDDEN! You disobeyed."

Rosie's heart melted in fear as the irate woman came closer. "What is THIS?" Her eyes burned with fire. She yanked the gold scarf from Rosie's neck and held it high above her head. "What are you doing with *this*? Why do you have it?"

Rosie stared in bewilderment. "I...I...found it."

"It's not yours! It's not to be touched—ever. It's sacred."

"But...but, why?" She shrank back and ducked her head as Nina came closer.

"WHY?" Nina screamed inches from her face. She glared at her, and then at the mess. Rosie flinched as Nina gritted her teeth and spat through pursed lips. Droplets of spit sprayed Rosie's face. "Because I said so, dummy. You will be PUNISHED!"

The girl lifted her arm to wipe her face when Nina swatted Rosie's head and then yanked her up from the floor by her hair. "Now get down to your room. And when you get there, take out all of your clothes and put them on your bed."

She pushed Rosie so hard she tripped down a few of the narrow steps. "GO, I said."

Expecting the black hole, she prepared herself for the worst. But when Nina came into her room, Rosie didn't expect the icy words that pierced her heart.

"You have to go. You're damaged and broken, and

GOOD. FOR. NOTHING." Nina's voice rose another decibel with each word. "I don't want you."

It stung like icicles hitting her in the face. Rosie felt frozen to the floor and could only stare back into the darkened mascaraed eyes. Her stomach hurt, as if she had been punched hard.

"You're worthless!" Nina screamed, shoving an empty garbage bag into her hands. She wadded up the gold scarf and threw it at the girl. "You might as well take this too. It's ruined now. You've stained your mother's sacred scarf with your tears." Nina's frown was fierce. "It was special once, but she spoiled it too," her words dripped with sarcasm and bitterness. "It's no good now."

Rosie stared blankly at the woman, dazed and confused. She couldn't move.

Nina slapped the girl on the head. "Did you hear what I said, klutz? Are you deaf too? Pack up your stuff and leave. Now!"

"But...but where...?" Her little body shook with sobs as she stuffed her few belongings into the bag.

"Anywhere. Just go." Nina shoved her out the door. "Get out. And don't come back."

Tears blurred her vision as she stood in the middle of the drive, unable to think or move. Rosie heard Nina get into her car and turn back toward the beach from which they had just returned. Slowly, putting one foot in front of the other, she began her journey down the road on that awful June afternoon.

Almost given to Benny. Kicked out by Nina. A scary ride with the old man until I got away. Hope and Faith were the only good that happened until I got taken away. And now, here I am waiting. But, for what? Rosie buried her head into her beloved scarf and wept. *Nina hated me, but I never dreamed she would throw me away.*

Why? What did I do wrong?

18 - THE GROUP HOME

It was three weeks into Rosie's stay at the emergency shelter. Rosie and Julie were about to put their trays on the counter after lunch when the day supervisor came up to her. "Rosie. Ms. Anders wants to see you."

"Lucky you." Julie stuck up her nose. "Bet you get to leave."

Rosie stood with trepidation outside Ms. Anders's office. Her body shook, making her leg feel as if it would give way.

"Come in, Rose," said Ms. Anders. "Sit down, I need to talk to you."

Rosie was suspicious of the social worker's pleasant voice; unexpected kind words had tricked her before. She pulled her sweater more tightly around her shoulders and sat on the edge of her seat. She waited in silence for Ms. Anders to speak.

"You will be moving to the Children's Home next week until we can find foster care for you. Get your things together," said Ms. Anders.

Rosie nodded and got up to leave. Ms. Anders motioned for her to stay seated. "I'm not finished yet, young lady."

Rosie shrank back onto her chair and pulled her

head into her neck. The few times she had gotten into trouble with Maddie made her worry. *Is Ms. Anders going to punish me—or take it out on Hope and Faith?* Rosie bit her lip and interlaced her fingers on her lap.

"I visited your home in Abbotsville. Looks like your Nina hasn't been there for a while. Your neighbor didn't know where she was either."

A shiver was visible as the girl looked at the floor, horror-stricken. *Then she doesn't know about Benny's place yet. If they find Nina, they might make me go back and live with her.*

"Do you know where she is, Rose?"

Rosie's face flushed. Her heart began to pound. Her folded hands were wet with sweat. Taking a deep breath, she looked into the caseworker's eyes. "No, ma'am." Her voice was quiet but determined. "Last time I saw her, she was driving away. Told me to get out 'cuz she don't want me." Rosie's shoulders sagged. "So I don't care where she is."

Ms. Anders rose and went over by the girl. Putting her hand on Rosie's shoulder, she gave a gentle squeeze. "I'm truly sorry, Rose. You're dismissed."

Rosie met Julie in the dining hall. "You're right. I'm going to the Children's Home. You been there?"

"Yeah. Nothing special. But at least you'll have a room with a door. You might have to share it with another girl."

"For how long?"

"No one knows. If they can't find any relatives to take you, then you go to the Home until they can find foster parents."

"Oh." The plate in Rosie's hand almost dropped to the floor. She steadied her hand to catch it before it broke. The worries began again.

Ms. Anders drove Rosie to the Children's Home the following Monday. After being registered, she said goodbye to Ms. Anders, and another lady took Rosie to her room.

"This is Kim. She arrived over the weekend. Put your clothes away and then meet me in the foyer in an hour," said the lady.

Rosie put her clothes in the dresser with a cautious eye on her new younger-looking roommate. After the incident with Maddie at the group home, she didn't want to risk having her beloved scarf stolen here. Rosie rolled the scarf as small as it would get, tucked it underneath her other clothes, and hoped it would be safe.

"Come on, slowpoke. We're gonna be late," Kim gave her a little push.

The invisible needles poking Rosie's bad leg from kneeling on the floor forced her to crawl to her bedside to pull herself up from her knees to stand.

"What's wrong with you?" asked Kim. "Ya lame or sumpthin'?"

"My leg just went to sleep. It's nothing."

Rosie hobbled more than usual as she followed the lady giving the tour. Kim liked the art room with all its easels, paints, books covering one whole wall, and lots of craft items on a long worktable. The last room made Rosie's heart leap for joy. A baby grand piano sat in the middle of the room with several other instruments and music stands resting here and there.

"Ooooh... " she pointed to the piano. "May I play it?"

"Of course," said the lady giving the tour.

"Ha. Like ya think ya can play?" Kim scoffed.

Rosie ignored Kim and sat down on the bench. Placing her fingers on the slick ivories, she first played a scale, and then picked a song from her head and found the melody on the keys.

"You have some talent," said the lady. "You can take piano lessons here, but unfortunately, we don't have a teacher right now. You can still sign up, though."

"I know a great piano teacher! Maybe she would come here to teach."

"Give the secretary the piano teacher's name when you sign up in the office, then," said the lady as she walked them to the dining room.

"The dining room looks like a restaurant," said Rosie. "Not like the picnic tables at the shelter."

Kim snubbed her. "Show-off," she sneered as they got their food.

"What do you mean?" Rosie felt the scorn.

"Trying to play the piano? Like you're smart or sumpthin'?"

"No," Rosie was offended. "I just..."

"Guess ya gotta do sumpthin' to take your mind off that monster bite."

"W-w-what?" Rosie put her hand over her scar, making it welt.

"Never mind. I'm sitting over there." Kim tossed her blond ponytail, lifting her nose at Rosie.

Why would she say that? Rosie found her own place by the window and wondered what to do next.

The next day, Rosie signed up for piano lessons and gave Hope's name to the secretary. She would practice and learn. She would have to learn to ignore Kim.

Kim's teasing and name-calling did not stop, but only worsened. The only place she felt relief was being alone with her music. The piano became her solace and the practice room her sanctuary.

A couple more weeks passed before the office gave Rosie a lesson time and day. Excited to learn how to read music, she hurried to the piano room. Her heart skipped a beat when she saw the new teacher waiting for her on the piano bench.

"HOPE!" she squealed in delight. She ran as quick as her leg would allow and threw her arms around the older lady.

Hope chuckled with pleasure as she hugged the girl in return. "I heard there was an opening for a piano teacher here! My, there were so many hoops to jump through. So glad I passed all their checks."

"Oh, Hope!" Rosie hugged her tight. "I've missed you so much."

"You know, when the lady took you from our home that day, I prayed God would make a way for me to see you again. And praise be! God always makes a way when you pray, little one. When the Home called me about teaching piano lessons, I hoped you'd be here, too. And here you are!"

"I'm so happy you came!"

"And you know the best part? I get to see you every week now! Praise be to God!" said Hope.

"I've been talking to God, too, just like you told me."

"One thing to remember, Rosie. God doesn't always do exactly what we ask, but we can count on Him to always do what's best. Have hope. Hold on to faith and trust."

"I will, Hope. I will."

19 – TROUBLES

Rosie made time every day to go to the piano room to tinker on the ivories, despite Kim's teasing. It became a refuge from Kim's taunts, and a place where she could be alone with her thoughts. Little by little, the songs built within her and overflowed onto the keys.

One day as she walked to the music room, her arms piled with music books, she didn't see Kim hiding in ambush. As she rounded the corner, Kim stuck out her leg causing Rosie to trip and sprawl on the hardwood floor. Music sheets and books flew out of her hands as she tried to break her fall.

"How was your trip, scarface? Have a nice fall?" Kim held her sides, laughing. "What a klutz. Hey! Want to go outside and jump rope with me? Oh, wait a minute, you can't." She gave Rosie a downward push as she passed her. "Later, loser."

The words stung. Rosie stretched to pick up her music and then picked herself up from the floor. She choked back the tears that threatened to come. *It's starting all over again.*

At her next piano lesson, Hope heard the whole story plus the many other times she had experienced troubles with Kim.

"What can I do?" asked Rosie. "She hates me, and she's so…so mean."

"Have you talked to anyone else about it?"

"No. She always does stuff when no one's looking so she won't get caught."

"Sound like she's a big bully," Hope said. "And she's your roommate, too?"

"Yeah. That makes it even worse. I hear it night and day. She makes fun of me when I read my Bible and pray, too."

"What do you do when she calls you names?"

"I pretend not to hear, and that it doesn't hurt, but it does." Rosie set up her music book for the lesson.

The woman put her stocky arms around the girl. "I know it does, honey. Maybe Kim has hurts of her own and is taking it out on you. Have you tried to be her friend?"

Rosie tilted her head, confused. "She wouldn't want to be my friend."

"Let's try an experiment. When the time is right, ask Kim about her story. Find out why she's at the Children's Home. If you're brave, maybe you could even ask why she's so mean to you. Think you can do that?"

The girl bit her lip, thinking hard. "I don't know…." She toyed with a few keys.

"The Bible tells us to be kind to one another. Try talking to her first. If your friendship and kindness won't make her stop teasing, then I'll go with you to the supervisor. Okay?"

Rosie stopped to twist her fingers, thinking about what to say. "How will I know when the time is right?"

"God will show you and you'll just know. He can give you the strength to do this. Let me pray for you now that He will give you the words to say to Kim. Trust Him to show you."

The girl released a heavy sigh. "Okay," not sure she truly understood.

The following week, Rosie went to her lesson, but Hope didn't show up. Wondering what happened, she asked the secretary in the office and was told Hope hadn't been feeling well. She had so much to tell her friend, she felt as if she would burst.

Two weeks later, Hope came early to Rosie's piano lesson, ready for another tearful event. Lesson times were becoming more like counseling sessions and life lessons rather than piano lessons.

Rosie bounced into the room all bubbly with a smile curved on her lips.

"Well, well! Look at you, child. You look mighty happy today."

Rosie giggled. "You'll never believe it," she said. "I

did like you said, Hope. I prayed all the way back to my room after last time. When I got there, Kim was sitting on her bed crying. I never saw her cry before. She always acts so tough."

"Was she hurt?"

"Hurting inside. I sat down beside her and asked her what was wrong. She had just come back from a home visit. She told me how her mom and dad were mean to her and called her names. We talked a long time."

"And that's why she was mean to you?"

"Uh-huh. She wanted to make me hurt like her. Said she was sorry about making fun of me, especially about my piano playing."

"You did a great job of being a friend, then."

Rosie tucked her head. "She actually said she wished she could play like me."

"You did the right thing, sweetie. You were kind to her, and it paid off."

After her lesson, Hope and she prayed together, like all other times. Rosie gave Hope a quick peck on the cheek, picked up her books, and prepared to leave. The music room door opened, and a blond-haired girl stepped in.

"I have a new student today," said Hope, motioning her to enter. "Looks like she's a little early."

Rosie's jaw dropped, and her lips curled into a

smile. “Hope, I want you to meet my new friend, Kim.”

20 - BENNY'S PLACE

John Flanders flipped the matchbook over in his hand as he set the GPS for the address to Benny's Place. He was anxious to see what kind of business this Benny had going.

On his forty-five-minute drive, Flanders fumed about old man Barnes's reactions when he had searched Rusty's house. *Nervous and fidgety. Smoked one cigarette after another. Barnes knew all along it was Rusty's house, not Carmen's. He knew Rosie too. How much is he really involved? I'll have a little talk with him once I'm done here.*

As he navigated toward the lakefront, Flanders expected to see the normal resort area: restaurants, hotels, cottages for rent, boat slips, walkways. He saw a sign pointing toward 'Benny's Place' on the waterfront of Table Rock Lake.

From the back view, he saw a run-down three-story building which appeared to be a hotel between fifteen to twenty years old. It needed a good painting and a new roof. He figured the upper floors were rooms for rent. Driving around to the front, he gawked at the neon flashing sign. *Should have guessed by the matchbook cover.*

His watch read 12:30 p.m. He parked his car in the lot with a few other cars. He walked up to the door. The sign read: OPEN: 5:00 p.m.-2:00 a.m. Apprehensive, he tried the door. It opened into a darkened room which appeared to be a restaurant with a bar area. Maybe once a well-furnished establishment with oak tables and velvet-covered chairs surrounding an open dance area, it was now simply old and run down and reeked of wine and cheap perfume.

Flanders went to the bar with its marred countertop and frayed, torn seats. On impulse he asked, “Rusty around?”

The barkeep gave him a sideways glance. “Not here.”

Flanders gave a slight nod. “When will she be back?”

“Don’t know. Margo is upstairs if you want her.”

“Uh...no. Only looking for Rusty. How about Benny? Is he here?”

The barkeep gave the man in the black business suit a suspicious stare. “Got an appointment?”

“No. Just dropping in. Want to surprise him.” He made reasons up as he spoke.

“Okay. Hold on. I’ll see if he’s free.”

Jackpot. He congratulated himself on an act well-played. There really is a Benny at ‘Benny’s Place’.

He decided to browse around the room while he waited. Photos of ladies decorated the walls. *Ladies of the night.* He stopped at the third photo that had a strange familiarity. *Where have I seen that redhead before?* The picture he'd seen at Rusty's house with the mother and child popped into his brain. *It's her. Rusty Delahunt, a red-haired beauty.* The photo next to it was a younger version: a beautiful teenage girl with long red hair in nothing more than simple bandeau and a gold scarf wrapped around her waist. He took out his phone and quickly snapped a few shots.

The manager approached Flanders from behind as he stood staring at the photos in the dimly lit room.

"They're beauties, aren't they? Especially Carmen," he pointed to the teenager. "She knew how to tease." He chuckled. "I was sorry when I lost her."

Flanders immediately recognized the voice and swung around to face Benny. "Well, well, well. Hello, Mr. Barnes."

Benny Barnes's face turned gray. "Detective! What are you doing here? How d'ya even—" He scratched his stubbled chin with a trembling hand.

"How did I find you? I'm a detective. That's what I do. I look for clues, and you left me some good ones."

Benny took a few steps back. "I run a reputable business here. I—"

Flanders stopped him mid-sentence by grabbing

his arm. "You know I could shut you down in a minute, Barnes. That's not what I'm here for today. Like I said before, I must find Rusty. And I think you know where she is."

Benny cleared his throat and laughed nervously. "I thought you were looking for Carmen."

"No, you didn't. You wanted me to believe Carmen was alive," Flanders' tone was harsh as he stared the man down. "You knew Rusty was the one I wanted all along. When she'll be back?"

"What makes you think she'll be back here?"

"Your barkeep told me she'd left for a while. So, I'll ask you again." He raised his voice. "*When* will she be back?"

Benny searched the ceiling for an answer. "I don't know, sir. Honest. She packed her bags and said she was going somewhere," he lied.

"Where?"

"How would I know?" Benny fumbled in his pocket for a cigarette.

"Because you know her, Barnes. From way back, I'm guessing by those photos on the wall. She was one of your 'employees', wasn't she?"

Benny twisted his neck and ignored the question. "Said she was visiting a friend."

"How about a phone number then?"

"Against house rules..."

"Would you rather I come back with a police warrant?" The detective gave him an evil eye.

With reluctance, Benny grabbed a napkin from one of the tables and wrote the number down.

"Good. Now. Tell me what you know about Rosie."

Benny sank down in a chair, took a long draw on his cigarette, and breathed it out slowly. "It's a long story, sir."

"I've got time."

"Okay. Here's what I know about the kid."

21 - ABOUT NINA

On the way back to Queen City, Detective Flanders called Hazel Walters. "I need to ask a few more questions, Mrs. Walters. May I come to see you?"

"You know I love to talk about my neighbors, Detective." She tittered. "Oh my, that came out wrong. Of course. You're welcome to come see me anytime."

Before he could ring the bell, Mrs. Walters opened the door.

"Come in, detective. I've baked a fresh pie. We can sit and chat for a while. I'm so happy to have good company."

Flanders rolled his eyes and followed her as she waddled to the kitchen. "It smells delicious, ma'am."

They chit-chatted a while before he could get to the crux of the matter. "I believe you gave me incorrect information last time I was here, Mrs. Walters."

"Whatever do you mean, sir?" Her bright eyes twinkled. "I told you what I knew. And please, call me Hazel."

"You led me to believe Carmen Delahunt lived across the street with her daughter, Rosie."

"Now, now. Did I say that?" Her smile was coy. "I figured you knew the lady you wanted was Rusty Delahunt, not Carmen." Hazel served him a piece of caramel apple pie. "Carmie died over ten years ago."

"See there? I knew you had a lot more information," said the detective. "So then, Rosie lived with Rusty?"

"Yes, Rusty was left to raise the child after Carmie died. Terrible state of affairs," said Hazel. She poured them cups of coffee and then sat down across from him.

"What happened to Carmen?"

"Well—" Hazel clucked her tongue. "Let me tell you a sad story—a sad one indeed." She took a bite of her pie and waited for his full attention.

"When Rusty moved in across the street with her daughter, it was news on the whole street. Carmen was around age sixteen, I would guess, and pregnant. I remember because I took them my famous nut bread. Everyone likes my nut bread."

He nodded but kept his head down.

"I figured Rusty needed a friend, and I tried my best to be one."

Flanders raised his eyebrows but didn't comment. "Was there a Mr. Delahunt?"

"No. Rusty was divorced. So, no. There was no Mr. Delahunt. In fact, I think Delahunt may have been her maiden name. Never talked much about Carmie's father so I didn't want to pry, and he never came around that I knew of. You know I don't like to poke my nose into other people's business."

The detective rolled his eyes. "What do you know about Carmen's death?"

"I was with Rusty when she got the call about the accident."

Detective Flanders hurriedly jotted notes with a quick hand. "Accident?"

"Yes. But I'm getting ahead of myself," Hazel said, sitting back in her chair. "More coffee?" She poured it before he could answer.

"Rusty was distraught when her daughter became pregnant so young. Rusty didn't want to be a grandmother at the age of thirty-five. Told me so herself. Anyway," she gave a long sigh, "Carmie finally gave birth to a beautiful baby girl with tons of curly black hair."

"Was the child deformed in any way?"

"Oh. No. No...that came later. Another piece of pie, Detective?"

He waved her off and patted his bloated stomach. "It was delicious. Really. I will take more coffee, though. Please...continue. Tell me about Carmen."

"Patience, young man. I'm getting there." She rose slowly, massaging her hip with one hand. Pouring him another cup of coffee, she continued. "Little Rosie was a spunky, mischievous little one. Such a delight. Then, one night, the sky dumped buckets of rain. Rusty got a call no one wants to get."

"—from the police?"

"No, from the hospital. Carmen had been in a horrible accident. Rusty called me at 3:00 a.m. asking me to go with her to the hospital in Queen City. Said Carmie had driven somewhere to see the baby's father. When she didn't come home, Rusty figured she stayed the night and wasn't too worried." She cupped her hand to her mouth. "She was a lot like her mother in that respect," she said as if telling a secret.

"Then she got the dreaded call from the hospital. They said Carmie had flipped her car and was in serious condition. Her child was injured too."

Detective Flanders nodded his assents and put in his uh-huhs, and um-hmms where needed. He kept taking notes, slurping his coffee.

"I rode to the hospital with Rusty. She was a mess when she saw Carmie—hardly recognizable. Black and blue everywhere, swollen..." Hazel sniffled, recalling the sight. It brought tears to her eyes once again. "It was horrible. Just horrible. Rusty couldn't handle it." She dabbed her eyes with the corner of her apron.

"When did Rosie come to live with her?"

"After a week or so, Rosie was released from the

hospital. Taking care of a toddler with a cast on her leg was more than Rusty wanted to handle. It became an unwelcome chore. Rusty never liked being tied down, and that child tied her down. She couldn't visit Carmie much." Hazel wagged her head. "To be truthful, I think she blamed the child for the accident. It was plain to everyone she didn't like little Rosie after that accident."

"Why do you say that?" asked Flanders.

"After Carmen died, I tried to go visit, but Rusty didn't want anything to do with me. She was never the same after the accident. It changed her. I stopped visiting soon after. I hardly ever saw Rosie around. She never played in the yard. Made me wonder where she was."

"What did Rosie call Rusty?" The detective wanted to hear it said.

"She called her Nina. Rusty never wanted the name of Grandma. 'Too young for that,' she told me. She didn't like 'Nina' either, but...."

"What about Rosie's father?"

"They never talked about the father of the child. I never pried. Perhaps she didn't know who the father was. There were always lots of men." The older woman winked. "If you know what I mean."

"One more question, and then I'll leave. Do you know Rusty's married name?"

She furrowed her brow and put her finger to her mouth. "Hmm... I think she once mentioned Gavotte. Yes," she nodded with assurance, "it was Gavotte."

Detective Flanders sucked in a deep breath at the recognition of the name. "Any relation to Raymond Gavotte, the former Mayor of Queen City?"

"Why, yes. I believe so." Her brown eyes lit up. "Raymond was her ex-husband's name."

"Thank you again, Mrs. Walters. You have been a wealth of information today." He gave her his card. "And please, if you think of anything else, please give me a call." The detective rose from his chair and headed toward the door. "Anything at all–please call."

"Hazel. Please, call me Hazel." She gave him another wink. "And please come for another visit soon."

Detective Flanders' head spun as he drove back to Queen City. He had a lot of ground to cover before he could find out where little Miss Rosie belonged. First, he would check county offices for the marriage records of Raymond Gavotte. If he located Raymond, he may be able to get a better lead on Rusty. Who was Benny, the other man in Rusty's life? And who and where was Rosie's father?

22 - A FRIEND FROM THE PAST

A few hours before Benny's Place opened for evening business, Rusty sat at the bar worrying about the recent events. Living and working with Benny at the brothel, engaging in illicit affairs, abandoning Rosie, not to mention her harsh treatment, could bring great trouble.

Rusty rubbed the hardened knots that had formed on the back of her neck. Her life was in chaos and she had created it. She knew it, but until now, she hadn't cared. The creak of the opening door made her look up. A tall elegant lady gracefully aging into her fifties entered. It took a few moments before Rusty recognized her.

"Pris? Pris Jones? Wow! Look at you! You could pass for a model from a fashion magazine. It's been ages. Looks like life has treated you good." Rusty rose to hug her long-time friend.

"Rusty! You're a welcome sight! Is Benny still here?"

"Yep. The gang's all here. Come, sit and chat. How long has it been?"

"Too long, my friend. And my name is Connery now." Pris took a seat at one of the nearby tables.

"Remember Mr. Tall, Dark, and Handsome? The one on the 'special' trip who said he was just traveling through?"

Rusty scratched her head for a clue, recalling days past, "Oh, yes—the 'business' man. The rich guy you drooled over when he came in, then guzzled drinks with—the one with the expensive black silk suit?"

Pris smiled widely as she dug her phone out of her clutch and flipped to her pictures.

"Handsome guy. He whisked you away, did he?"

Pris Connery giggled. "Well, yes he did, my friend. After giving him a good night on the town a few times, he asked me to marry him. So, I did. He treated me good."

They caught up on life from their younger, reckless days working at Benny's. "We had some good times, didn't we?" Pris commented, viewing the pictures on the wall.

"Wild and wooly," laughed Rusty, glad to take her mind off her problems.

"Carmen was the looker," Pris pointed to the young teen framed on the wall. "How *is* your daughter? The last I remember, she was dancing for all the men. A young beauty with all that gorgeous red hair."

A thin smile crossed Rusty's lips for only a moment, and then quickly faded. "We've lost touch, haven't we, since our early days? So, so long ago...." Her voice went low. "My daughter is gone now."

"Grown up, I suspect."

Rusty tossed her head as if to free it from the past. She ran her fingers through her hair. "We have much to catch up on, but, another time. So, what brings you here?" Rusty went behind the bar to get them a couple of sodas.

"Ummm. Thanks," said Pris as she took the glass. "I've come back to get some things in order since my husband died. I'm staying at the Chateau over in Branson. Been following a Texan showman around the Midwest the last couple of years."

"Ooooh, I see...." Rusty flashed a grin. "High-dollar gal."

Pris giggled. "No, it's not like that–I mean, we're—well, close acquaintances, I suppose. He travels all over performing live shows. Quite good at it, I'll say. When I first saw posters around Little Rock, I attended out of curiosity. After the show, I saw him at a bar hiring people for the next night. It looked like fun, and I signed up. He liked my act, so I've become a regular. I have the money to travel, and it's enjoyable."

"What do you have to do?"

"Well, that's the fun and simple part," Pris explained. "All I have to do is answer 'yes' to everything he asks. I must look surprised, like he's really reading my mind. When he touches my forehead, I must pretend to faint. 'Just fall backward,' he told me, 'and someone will be there to catch you.' After I lay on the floor for a few minutes, I get back up and act like I'm in a daze. It sounded amusing, so I agreed to do it. I wear a red dress and put a white rose in my hair, so he can locate me easier. It's great!" Pris laughed. "Why don't you come see me in action?"

"It sounds crazy!" Rusty scoffed. "What's in it for you?"

"Just a little action and some fun, plus I get paid."

"What did you say his name was?"

"J.D., I think. J.D. - something. Oh, come on. What you need is to get out again. You're rusty, Rusty." She laughed at her own pun. "It will be good for you to get out. What do you say? Come with me?"

"Oh, okay." Rusty gave in.

"Great!" Pris gave her a quick squeeze. "I'll save you a place on the back row."

23 - THE SHOW

"J.D.'s HOUR OF POWER! THE LAME WALK-THE BLIND SEE! WITNESS MIRACLES HAPPEN" declared the posters. Blacart grinned as he drove through the town. The people of Branson had advertised well.

People followed J.D. Blacart everywhere. Invalids lined the aisles, hoping for a touch from the 'Man with the Golden Hands' and their chance for healing. His reputation was well known throughout the Midwest, holding his meetings from one town to the next. Crowds swarmed his evangelistic trail to see the signs and wonders performed by his hands. J.D. was good at his trade–a master magician pretending to be a preacher. He wooed them and wowed them and then raked in the crops. A few deceptions here, a couple of tricks and sleights-of-hand there, and people thought they had witnessed a miracle.

It worked perfectly, as he had planned. Blacart had become an icon for his charisma and long healing lines. The publicists declared, "When he touches someone, the miraculous happens." With a knack for persuasion, he believed he could sell anything–including God's power.

Blacart congratulated himself. He'd become a skilled orator who knew how to persuade and charm. He put on an act, became rich and famous, and lived his wild and shady lifestyle, and no one was the wiser.

The Branson meetings started out with a bang. J.D. smirked as he spotted performers placed strategically throughout the crowded tent. A man entering with sunglasses and a cane found his spot on the front row. He. spotted Priscilla Connery in her apple-red dress with the white rose in her hair. She caught his eye and gave a small wave of her hand. Nodding his head in recognition, he took note of her seat in the back. Checking where all his other actors were seated, he took his place on the platform. A sneer escaped Blacart's lips. Everything had been set up nicely, and he looked forward to a very profitable week.

Rusty found Pris and scooted in beside her. She jumped as a loud squeal from the microphone sent a chill up her back. The people erupted in applause and jumped to their feet as the song leader took over with high-spirited songs.

The charismatic preacher in his rhinestone-studded suit jumped to the microphone, grabbed it from its stand and shouted. "Are you ready to see the power of God?" He ran across the platform with the mike making it screech in his hand. "I said—are you ready to see the POWER of GOD?"

The crowd went wild. Rusty stretched her neck to see everything from the back. The preacher man proclaimed God's love but Rusty felt estranged from the love that had once been a part of her childhood. A deeply hidden spot in her heart tugged at her soul.

Scratching the old memories from her head as the preacher danced his way across the stage, she remembered Grandmom Delahunt. *Grandmom prayed about everything. She told me she prayed for me every night.* She missed the godly woman who used to take her to Sunday School. *She taught me right from wrong. I simply chose to do wrong. When I wanted my own way, I did my own thing. It led me... where?* She shook her head as her mind swirled down the gutter of her life.

I once had it all. Her heart pinged with a twinge of guilt. *A wonderful, rich, and reputable husband, a beautiful mansion to live in, and a darling baby girl.* Rusty clenched her jaw. *If only Benny wouldn't have come back.* She moaned.

Her thoughts drifted back to twenty years earlier when Benny found her in the park....

He had snuck up behind her as she sat on a blanket watching little Carmen play. Kneeling quietly, he wrapped his arms around her and squeezed tight.

"Rusty. My dear, dear Rusty."

"Benny? Is it really you? She pushed back from him and turned around to get a better look. "My! How you've changed!" Her eyes took in the vision of manliness before her. He had put on a few pounds but still had the blond Norwegian hair and hard-as-rock muscle in all the right places. Those clear-blue eyes melted her heart and his large toothy grin made her smile.

"You're more gorgeous than I remembered, Rusty."

She blushed, embracing the comment. "Aw, Benny, why do you always call me Rusty?" She gave him a pinch on the cheek.

"It's those red curls, doll. You know I've always been a sucker for a dame with red hair," he chuckled.

"And I've always admired a man with muscle." She squeezed Benny's bulging arm. "You're my knight in shining armor, Benny. What brings you to Queen City?"

"I needed to see you, Rusty. I want you to come back to me. Let it be like it was before."

"But I'm a married woman now and I have a daughter." She pointed to little Carmen on the swings.

"I know. Married to Raymond Gavotte, of all people." Benny spat at the ground.

"He's a good man."

"You mean a rich man. You married him for the money, Rus', admit it."

"Aw, Benny," she chortled, stroking his smooth tanned cheek. "He takes good care of me."

"I've seen how he takes care of you. I've seen the mansion you live in, the car you drive. I see how you dress." He let out a low whistle. "You love his money, that's all. You love the fame and fortune, but do you love him?"

"Sure..." she hesitated, "I think... I love him—" She paused with a skeptical frown.

"The way you loved me?"

Benny rose from the blanket and pulled Rusty up close to him. Putting his arms around her waist, he hugged her tightly, breathing heavily into her hair. She quivered in his embrace and melted into his arms, awakening more inside of her than she thought possible.

The hot, muggy Missouri breeze drifted across her face bringing her back to the present in this crazy tent meeting. Rusty squirmed at the repugnant memory and the downward path it had led her. The preacher man was saying something about your sins coming home to roost. It struck her conscience. Benny had been her downfall, but she had been a willing participant. It had cost her dearly. *If only Benny hadn't come back...*

Rusty's skin prickled when the preacher man shouted into the mike: "TONIGHT, IS YOUR NIGHT!"

Pris poked her in the side. "Show's starting," she whispered.

"You, on the front row with the checkered suit," Blacart called to the actor sitting in the front. "Come, receive your blessing tonight."

The middle-aged man made his way to the front pacing his white cane from side to side. Rusty watched in fascination as Blacart removed the man's sunglasses and rubbed his eyes with something oily. Tipping the man's face upward, he shouted, "Sir, tonight is YOUR night! Proclaim your sight!"

All at once, the man opened his eyes wide, threw down the cane and yelled out, "I can see! I can see!" He began to run around the aisles, shouting. "See what he did? J.D. healed me!"

Rusty tapped Pris on the arm. "Wait. Isn't that George from the pub?"

"Don't know. Could be. He hires people from everywhere."

"George isn't blind."

"Of course, he isn't. That lady isn't an invalid," she pointed to the plump lady with the walker, "and I'm not sick either." Pris giggled. "It's just a show!"

"Ma'am–back there," said Blacart into the

microphone, "you in the red dress."

Pris pointed to herself in question, acting surprised to be called up front. "Here we go," she whispered.

"Yes, you! Something special will happen for you tonight. Come forward."

Pris walked up front with her small hand over her mouth, looking timidly from side to side. When she stood before Blacart, Rusty saw her shiver in anticipation.

"I sense you are having stressful times," he said, his lapel mike broadcasting the conversation.

"Yes, yes I am."

"Are you also having stomach pains that are not going away?"

"Why, how did you know? Yes, I am."

"And you suspect it may be ulcers... or worse?"

"Yes!" Pris feigned a cry. She managed to eke out a tear.

"Tonight, you will be healed. This is YOUR night!" the preacher said.

"Yes. YES!" She threw her hands in the air in excitement.

Blacart put his hands on her stomach and moved his lips inaudibly. Then he gave her a tap to the forehead. Pris toppled over backward, straight into the arms of two strong ushers placed behind her, ready to break her fall. She lay on the floor with her eyes closed as if passed out.

Blacart let out a wild whoop, ran across the platform, and then called a few more up to the front.

Something's not right. Rusty fumed and squirmed in her seat. *It's deception and manipulation.* Her fists clenched into tight balls turning her knuckles white. *He shouldn't be fooling around with the power of God.*

"Well? How did I do?" Pris asked as they sat down for drinks afterward.

"You were quite the actress, Miss Pris. Do you really believe anything this guy says?"

"Not a word." Pris let out a hearty laugh. "He's just a showman. Always has been." She took a sip of her drink.

"Something about him looked familiar."

"Well, he could have been here another time. He's been all around the Midwest doing shows for years. He frequents all the pubs and taverns around the area too. That's where he finds most of his actors."

Rusty shook her head in shock. "But it's pure mockery." Her skin crawled.

"Since when did you get religion?" mocked Pris.

"It's still wrong." *Someone should expose him.*

24 - THE MAYOR

The marriage records showed Raymond Gavotte and Rozlyn Delahunt had married in Queen City almost thirty years before. Divorce papers revealed they'd been together for two years. He hoped Raymond Gavotte would know about Rusty's whereabouts. It took extensive research, but he finally tracked down the former mayor of Queen City living at the Resthaven Senior Residential Care on the south side of the city.

An aide ushered Flanders into the community room where he was to meet with Gavotte. He found Raymond sitting beside the large bay window gazing outside. The detective was surprised to find the once well-to-do and highly influential mayor confined to a wheelchair.

"Mr. Gavotte, I'm Detective John Flanders of Queen City Investigative Services. Thank you for giving me a little of your time."

The gentleman, who appeared to be in his sixties, turned his wheelchair halfway around to face the detective. "No problem, Mr. Flanders. Pull up a chair and sit. So, how can I help you today?"

"If you don't mind me saying so, I'm a little

surprised to see a man with your influence and expertise in a senior residential center."

"With no other living relatives nearby, I decided to get the best all-around care available. I can afford to live here where they take good care of me and still work as a legal consultant from time to time. Although my legs are immobile," he said, adjusting the blanket on his lap, "my mind still works," He chuckled. "Plus, I don't have to clean my room or do dishes."

"I see." Flanders grinned. He understood.

"This is my favorite place in the whole facility." Mr. Gavotte pointed out the window. "See those lovely flowers and the bird house? I love watching the birds. Those Eastern Bluebirds are my favorite–state bird of Missouri, did you know?"

The detective nodded and slid the chair up beside him. After small chit-chat, he dug out his notepad. "I'll get to the point, Mr. Gavotte." Clicking on his recorder, he asked, "Do you know Carmen Delahunt?"

Raymond's eyes lit up with recognition, but his face revealed stark sadness. He nodded. "Yes. Many, many years ago. Yes. I knew Carmen when she was a little girl."

The detective nodded and marked his notebook. "And what about Rusty Delahunt? I assume you know her too?"

The look of sadness on Gavotte's face turned to

disdain. "Yes. Of course. She's from my past. Still in trouble?"

"I need to locate her. Thought you could help."

"Sorry, I lost contact with her years ago."

"What can you tell me about her?"

Mr. Gavotte's blue eyes stared out the window, watching a bird flutter into the bird house. A sadness enveloped his weathered face. Taking a deep breath, he said, "Do you have some time, Detective?"

"Of course, please take your time."

"Good, because I have a story to tell you about Rusty Delahunt. I met Rusty, given name Rozlyn, Delahunt soon after she graduated high school. She was a saucy, red-haired beauty who turned everyone's head in her younger days."

He stared out the window, smiling at the memory. It quickly faded as he continued. "She ran with a rowdy crowd who knew her as Rusty. Quite a wild filly. I was twelve years older, born into a rich, influential family near the Kansas border. She served as a waitress at a social event I attended in Queen City. She flirted with me and when I gave her a wink, she seemed to fall for me head over heels. As I think back, I think she was the one who hooked me. Rozlyn knew my social status and wealth. Gavotte was an influential name in the community. I wasn't disabled then." He patted his legs. "We had a whirlwind engagement and were married within a few months." He grew quiet in thought and closed his eyes as memories returned afresh.

Detective Flanders hurriedly jotted notes.

"I had inherited the elegant Gavotte family mansion in Queen City when my father died. As the wife of the newly elected Mayor of Queen City, Rozlyn enjoyed the role of the First Lady, hosting parties and planning events. I supplied well for her and thought she loved me. Now I think she only loved the wealth of the Gavotte family. A few months into the marriage, Rozlyn became pregnant."

"Carmen?" the detective interrupted. Flanders recalled the picture he snapped from the house of the young woman with a baby–both with red hair.

Gavotte nodded and continued. "A couple of years later, things started taking a turn for the worse. The days of peaceful living were few and far between, especially after the accident."

"Accident?" asked the detective looking up from his notes. "Your legs?"

Gavotte adjusted the lap blanket over his legs and gazed out the window. "Yes. During a skiing trip, I crashed into a tree. It damaged my spinal cord and rendered me a paraplegic."

"How did that affect your term as mayor?"

"The city let me graciously finish my term in office,

but I chose not to run again. Being confined to a wheelchair proved to be too hard to perform my mayoral duties, make speeches, and all the rest that came with the office. I chose to put my legal background into consultant work instead."

"Did the accident affect your marriage to Rozlyn?"

"Yes. It changed her. I couldn't perform in the way she needed." Gavotte's eyes grew watery as he gazed out the window. He cleared his throat and continued. "There was gossip of Rozlyn entertaining male strangers at the mansion. Whenever I brought up the subject, she rose into a wild fury; accused me of judging her. She became a fiery demon out of hell when contradicted or confronted. Her rage knew no mercy."

"You accused her of being unfaithful?"

Gavotte's gaze grew distant as he traveled into the past. "I found my Irish redhead also had an ugly, mean streak in her. We grew farther apart by the day and we both knew it, yet, she would not admit to wrongdoing. One day as she got ready for a party, I made an idle comment about the evening gown she wore. Said it was too fancy for meeting with old friends. She claimed it was a formal affair."

He stopped and shook his head. Gavotte's voice became hoarse, and he began to cough. "Would you mind getting me a drink, sir?" He pointed to the water cooler. “Paper cups are in the cabinet to the right.”

Flanders obliged.

After taking a long drink of cold water, he asked, “Do you really want to hear this?”

“Whatever you wish to share, Mr. Gavotte. I’m ready to listen.”

He nodded and continued. “When Rozlyn put on my grandmother’s blue sapphire necklace, an heirloom and my wedding gift to her, along with her diamond earrings, I felt she’d stepped over the line. I told her what I thought, and she stormed out the door in an angry huff.”

His voice grew quieter at the memory. Digging out his handkerchief, he continued. “She didn’t come home until 3:00 a.m. I heard her stumbling in the kitchen. When she came into the bedroom, I smelled liquor on her breath. Her hair was askew, necklace gone, and an earring missing. I didn’t like what my heart told me.”

“Mr. Gavotte, if you’re uncomfortable telling me all this—”

“No. You must know everything. You must know the way she was....” Gavotte coughed into his handkerchief and continued. “And how she got to be the way she is.”

25 - BAD DREAM

Rusty tossed and turned on her bed after witnessing the deception at the tent crusade. She couldn't get J.D. Blacart out of her head. In restless sleep, she dreamed of a tall, muscular cowboy with a chiseled jaw and smooth tongue which made her and Pris quiver. They ogled him with flirtatious smiles as he entered the bar. He savored their gaze and tipped his large Stetson with a sly smile.

Rusty sauntered to his table in the darkest corner of the room and put sugar in her voice. "Hi there, handsome. You're just in time for the live show," she whispered, "they're all here to see *her*."

Rusty's sleep became sweaty anguish. Sheets tangled about her body as she writhed in bed at the disturbing dream.

The cowboy sat and watched, keeping his face in the dark. The music slowed as the lights dimmed to low. Slender and sleek, a young girl in her mid-teens entered the dance floor from the back hall, passing directly in front of the cowboy. Bending, turning, the dancer submitted her body to the will of the music. As the resonance heightened and tempo quickened, she dipped and glided to each table. Her moves mesmerized the watchers.

But she danced only for him.

Rusty saw the look in the man's eyes. She'd seen it before. He was smitten–and hooked. After the night's performance as they were preparing for bed, Rusty squeezed her girl.

"You were very alluring tonight, Carmie."

"Thanks, Mama. Everything I know, I learned from you!"

Drenched with sweat and tears, Rusty awoke and choked on her own spit. *Everything I know, I learned from you.* The words burned in her head and struck her heart.

The vision of J.D. Blacart preaching hell, fire, and brimstone came back to her remembrance. Suddenly all the dots connected to the cowboy in her dreams. The man in the Stetson was none other than J. D. Blacart.

Rusty arose and quickly pulled on her clothes. She knew now what she had to do.

In the residential home on the south side of Queen City, Detective Flanders continued his conversation with the former mayor of the city.

Raymond Gavotte took a deep breath and went on with his story about the lady he once called his wife. "For the next few months, Rozlyn snuck out on a regular basis to meet secretly with her old boyfriend. I learned about her affair one day after receiving an unmarked envelope on my desk. It held the missing necklace and earring. No note, no name."

"Did you ask around?"

"Yes, but no one admitted to putting it there. A few weeks later, a coworker apologetically told me he'd seen Rozyln at the pub with another man. He didn't go into much detail, but he didn't have to. I got the picture. It made me furious. Detective, I was distraught and bewildered." His face and neck grew red at the memory. He began to cough again. "Sorry."

"Let me get you some more water, sir," the detective rose.

"Thank you. It's just that...."

"You don't have to go on. I can see you had good reason to be upset."

"Upset? Upset wasn't even close. I was mad enough to spit nails. Should have known all along, but I chose to remain ignorant. I slammed the jewelry down on the coffee table in front of my wife that very night and demanded to know where she'd left them. I wanted her to admit it. 'We're Gavottes,' I told her.

'Gavottes do not do such things. We're a proper family. You are the Mayor's wife. You have an image to uphold, and it's not gallivanting with drunkards.'" He grew husky with emotion.

"Did she admit it?"

"No! She denied it. I called her a liar. Too many people had seen her. Told her I would not let her ruin our family name or my reputation. I would not have a scandalous wife in my house. Then," Gavotte paused to take another drink, "I told her to leave. Later that evening, I heard Rozlyn call Benny for help. She packed her bags and was gone with Carmen the next morning."

Mr. Gavotte choked up as he finished his story, coughing into his handkerchief. The man slumped in his wheelchair and emptied his cup of water. The detective gave the man a few minutes to pull himself together while he threw the paper cup in the trash.

"Thank you for sharing your story, Mr. Gavotte. I know it was hard to tell, but it helps me to know the woman now known as Rusty Delahunt."

"So, she took back her maiden name. That's a good thing–at least she didn't drag the Gavotte name into her stinking sewer. Her lover called her Rusty."

"Was that Benny Barnes?"

"Yes."

"Did you ever try to contact Rusty, uh, I mean

Rozlyn?"

"No. I couldn't." He hesitated, "and because of my pride, I wouldn't."

"Weren't you curious about your daughter, Carmen?"

"I sometimes wondered if she was really my child after I found out about Rozlyn's affairs. Carmen was only two when Rozlyn left. She never brought her to see me, and I never tried to see her either."

"Why not?"

He exhaled deeply and shook his head. "At that point in my life, I guess I didn't care. My anger and my pride overpowered me. My job was overwhelming and kept me busy...and..." He dabbed his eyes. "I guess there's no real excuse, sir. I just didn't. Maybe there's still a chance to find my daughter?"

"I'm sorry to be so blunt, but Carmen's dead. Certainly, you must have known?" said Flanders. "She died in a car accident at the age of eighteen."

Gavotte's eyes widened. "No. I didn't know. Rozlyn even kept that from me. It may have been headline news in the smaller towns, but not here."

"Sorry to be the one to break the news."

"Guess when I told Rozlyn to get out of my sight, she took it literally."

Flanders checked over his notes, and then asked, "Did she ever try to come back?"

"Once Rozlyn tried to say she was sorry. She wanted me to take her back and forgive all. But I knew her; she would not change her lifestyle. I would not—could not forgive her."

"What kind of lifestyle?"

"Prostitution—at Benny's. He runs an 'establishment', if you will."

The detective raised his eyebrows with an affirmative nod. "When did she ask you to take her back?"

Gavotte scratched the memory from his silvery hair, "Ah...let me see," he closed his eyes to think. "It would have been about twelve years or so ago. I didn't believe she was sincere. Suspected she only wanted my money."

Flanders counted the years in his head. "Sorry to say, it looks like your daughter followed in her mother's footsteps."

Gavotte stared blankly at the news.

"Mr. Gavotte..." the detective began slowly, "...did you know Carmen gave birth to a little girl twelve years ago?"

"No. I did not." Realization dawned on his face. "Where is she now? Living with Rozlyn?"

"No. She is safe for the time being with Child Protective Services, soon to move to foster care."

Gavotte had a look of relief as he let out a huge

breath. "Good. I'm glad she's not with Rozlyn. Please, Detective. Don't let her know about me. I couldn't bear to have her see me this way."

"But that's why I still need to locate Rozlyn—to settle things for the girl's sake. Do you have any clue to where Rozlyn is now?"

Raymond Gavotte shook his head. "My guess? With Benny." He rubbed his paralyzed legs and stared outside as another bird fluttered nearby. "Maybe if I would have taken Rozlyn back when she asked, or never kicked her out in the first place, things would have been much different today. I have much to regret."

"Should 'a. Could 'a. Would 'a. But now you have a granddaughter, Mr. Gavotte. You still have a chance to make things right for Rosie."

"Rosie..." he tumbled the name around his tongue.

26 – CLUES

Stacey Anders sat at her desk, tapping the pen to paper. She faced a problem. The most ideal situation for an abandoned or runaway child was to place him or her with a relative until things were worked out with the parents or guardians. If there was no relative found, then the child was put into a group home or foster care as soon as possible. In Rosie's case, there were no other relatives, except for 'Nina', whoever she was, and she was running somewhere in the wind.

Ms. Anders pulled several folders looking for suitable foster parents for Rosie. As she thumbed through the names, the Davis's name seemed to jump out. A strange feeling overcame her. She shrugged it off and kept looking, but the name kept popping back into her head. She pulled their file and read: *prefer ages 0-5. Hmm...Rose is twelve.* She decided to call them, anyway. *Hurts nothing to call.* She tapped in the number and after several rings, Jim Davis answered.

"Hello. This is Stacey Anders from Child Protective Services. I'm calling to ask you about temporary child placement."

"Oh, yes!" answered Jim Davis. "We've been

waiting for this call. Mary will be thrilled! We have the nursery ready to go."

"Well, that may be a problem. This girl is twelve, not a baby. I know your files say you prefer ages newborn to five, but for some reason, your name kept coming back to me. I really believe you and Mary would be the perfect fit due to your social status, at least temporarily. You have no other children, so you could give this girl your full attention."

"I see." There was a long pause on the other end of the line. "Can you give me her background?"

"Sure. We're treating her as a runaway. We're not sure of her complete background because we haven't been able to locate any relatives yet. She has a few physical disabilities and some anxiety but is really a sweet girl. She shouldn't be a behavioral problem."

Another long pause.... "I'll have to discuss it with my wife."

"I understand completely. If she agrees, could you convert the nursery into a girl's bedroom?"

"Yes, it's possible. I'll call you back with our decision."

Almost as soon as she hung up, the telephone rang.

"Ms. Anders? Great news!" Detective Flanders said. "I found out who Nina is." The detective went on to tell her about his conversation with Hazel Walters, Benny Barnes, and Raymond Gavotte.

"So..., Ms. Anders pondered. "*This* is 'Nina.' The woman who tossed Rosie out on the street was none other than her own grandmother?"

"Appears so. Rusty Delahunt and the once-esteemed Rozlyn Gavotte are one and the same."

"It hardly seems possible," commented Ms. Anders. "Why would she run from that illustrious lifestyle? Returned to her wild past, perhaps?"

"Yeah, her ex-husband told me quite the story. She had her reasons. He thinks she's still with Benny. Benny's not telling but I was able to get Rusty's cell phone number from him."

27 – CONFESSION

Her reflection told her she needed another dye job. Her graying roots revealed too much of her age. She swooped her hair back and secured it with a rubber band. With new purpose, Rusty resolved to do something right for once in her life.

"Pris," Rusty called her friend. "How much longer will the preacher be in Branson?"

"Only one more day, I think. Why?"

"Let's say I have a few loose ends to tie up. And you said he's staying at the Chateau too?"

"Ah...yeah," she hesitated. "What's going through that head of yours, Rus'?"

"Well...," She hesitated. "Do you have time to talk?"

"Sure. Can you come over here? Atrium Café?"

"Be there in a few minutes." With new vigor, Rusty pulled out pen and paper and began to write. After several wadded-up sheets landed in the trash, she was finally satisfied with her words. She folded the letter, put it in an envelope, printed the name on the outside, and stuck it in her bag. Heading southeast on the back roads, she was anxious to get this heavy load off her chest.

She dropped the envelope off at the reception desk of the Chateau and then met Pris in the attached Atrium Café.

"Let's sit at one of the back tables, out of earshot."

"What are you up to, Rus'?" Pris asked again, showing alarm at Rusty's insistence of privacy.

After ordering sandwiches and sodas, Rusty lowered her voice. "This man–this J. D.—is a fraud. He's deceiving people."

Pris laughed out loud. "I know that. Everybody knows that."

"No–not all people do. Many are believers who have a real faith. They want to believe God really heals these people. Grandmom had faith like that. There is such a thing as the real thing. But this guy is a manipulator and a deceiver. He is lying and tricking these poor people into giving money to him." Rusty paused to take a long sip of her soda. "Did you see all the trinkets he had for sale? He's fleecing the flock."

"He's what?" Pris wrinkled her forehead as she wiped a dab of mayo from her mouth.

"People support his deception and don't even realize it. They empty their pockets for his gain. I'm going to EXPOSE him for the fake he is. And do you want to know something else?" Rusty's voice raised a notch with each word, startling the passing waiter.

His tray crashed to the floor, sending plates and glasses shattering everywhere. Both ladies jumped. Pris put a finger over her lips.

Rusty mouthed the waiter an 'I'm sorry' and took a bite of her sandwich. Lowering her voice, she spoke through the food in her mouth. "He's the father of Carmie's child!"

Pris's mouth dropped open. "Wha-a-at? Now you have my full attention. You have a grandchild?"

"Yeah. I guess that's what you'd call her." Rusty gritted her teeth.

Pris frowned at the reply. "And where's Carmie now? You said before she was gone. Gone, where?"

Rusty wilted at the question. "Oh...Pris." Her voice got quiet again. "You couldn't have known. You were gone from Benny's Place by then. My Carmen is dead. She passed over ten years ago."

The memories were so painful, pushed from her mind for so long, that Rusty had hardened into a calloused shell. Seeing Pris again brought the raw emotions to the surface. She couldn't hold back any longer. Rusty winced and continued. "You remember the day the young Texan came to the pub over a decade ago? The one we both drooled over?"

Pris leaned back and looked at the ceiling for a hint. "Ah, yes. I do remember, the tall drink of handsome with curly black hair and piercing black eyes?" She licked her lips. "He was a looker."

"I dreamed last night how Carmie enticed him—as if it were happening all over again."

"I do remember that night," remembered Pris. "Carmen's steps were deliberate as she slowly untied the gold scarf from her waist and then held it high. So graceful. She knew how to use that scarf to her advantage, making it float through the air in rhythm to the music. And then she let it drift across his face.

"Carmie taunted him. Seduced him. It was plain to see. She was doing everything I taught her." Rusty sighed, pinching the bridge of her nose.

Pris took another bite of her club sandwich. "Um-hmm."

Benny liked how she brought in the men. "'Everything I know, I learned from you,' she told me. She thought she was so in love with Jon, and so sure he loved her too. But when he left town, she never saw him again."

"Let's walk. I want to hear the whole story," said Pris as they paid their bills.

They headed toward Moonshine Beach, a block or so from the Chateau on Table Rock Lake. Pris breathed in the lake air and cocked her head at the seagull's cries. Taking off her sandals, she dug her toe into the sand. "About the scarf...you gave her that for her sixteenth birthday that very night, didn't you?"

Rusty moaned with the memory. "Yes, the scarf was meant to be a legacy handed down to each generation. Grandmom made it. She said she wove a prayer into every stitch and said it would bring great blessings to whoever wore it. My grandmom used to put it around her head when she prayed. I got it as an heirloom on my sixteenth birthday and kept it to wrap Carmie in when she was born. On her sixteenth birthday, she received the legacy."

Pris let out a rueful laugh. "It didn't work so well for Carmie, did it? The blessings stuff, I mean."

"Guess I never told her Grandmom's story, but I didn't believe in any of that stuff by then. Figured Carmie could do whatever she wanted with it. After she died, I boxed it and put in a trunk, never wanting to see that cursed scarf again."

"Carmie never thought about getting pregnant, never thought about the future...never thought, period. She only lived for the moment, living on love–until he left. And then Carmie found she was pregnant. That was close to thirteen years ago now, come this September." The pain etched her face.

"And he didn't know about the baby? Are you sure it was his child?"

"Carmie had that man coming back every night to see her. And the girl looks like him. But no. He vanished, so he was never aware. Carmie searched for

Jon several months but couldn't find him anywhere."

"How did Carmie die?" Pris dared to ask.

"He used her," she gritted her teeth, "... abused her, and then killed her."

28 – BLAME

"Killed her? The preacher?" Pris was aghast.

Rusty wiped her eyes. "Well, he didn't actually murder her, but he killed her all the same in my eyes. A couple of years passed, and Rosie was almost two years old. Carmie saw posters around town advertising the preacher. She was excited because she recognized Jon. 'He's famous,' she told me. She wanted to show him his child. She believed he would be so happy to have a daughter and love her all the more. Carmie dreamed he would take her away and they would live happily ever after. She was a child with a child living in a fairytale dream."

"Did she see him? Did he recognize her?"

"I don't know. His meeting was a few hours away. Carmie put Rosie in the car and took off to see him. Later that night, the hospital called to say she was in a terrible car accident. They found the wreckage down the side of a ravine. Demolished. She was thrown through the windshield. Rosie was trapped in her car seat. It was a wonder both weren't killed outright. We waited for weeks to see if Carmie would come out of her coma. Finally, the doctor gave me no choice. I had to be the one to tell them to pull the plug. She was brain dead." Rusty's voice caught. "She was only eighteen years old! I let her die..." Rusty put her hand to her heart. "But HE killed her."

They walked a while in silence as Rusty bore the pain all over again.

"What about the child?" Pris asked in barely a whisper.

"Carmie tried to pacify me by naming her after me and my ex-husband–Rosalita Rae. It didn't make me happy. I was angry." She kicked at the sand.

"But now you have a granddaughter. Does she look like you and her mother with silky red hair and fair skin?"

"No!" Rusty spat the word. "She looks like her father. Dark. Black curly hair. Piercing black eyes."

"Then she must be gorgeous," Priscilla mused out loud.

"She's scarred. . . and crippled. . . and I couldn't stand to look at her."

"Rusty! That's cruel!"

"I don't care. That's how I felt," Rusty tightened her lip.

"You speak of her as if she were in your past, too," Pris's voice held concern. "Where is she now, Rus'?"

Rusty's face turned into a bitter frown. She swiped at her face with a rough hand. "I don't know. She's gone, too."

Pris looked surprised. "Gone?"

"I kicked her out when I went back to Benny. I don't know where she went." Rusty picked up a rock and threw it at the water. "And I don't care."

"RUSTY! How can you say that? Not care? Not know where she is?"

"She disgusted me. Every time I looked at Rosie, I thought of the wretched man who ruined my Carmie. I resented him. Instead of taking home my daughter after the accident, I was left with a crippled child to raise. It wasn't fair. It's all her fault. If she wouldn't have been born, none of this would have happened." Rusty fell to her knees in the sand, putting her hands to her neck. Her icy words even stung her own throat.

Pris put her hand over her mouth, startled at Rusty's outburst. She stood staring at her friend at a loss for words. After a couple of minutes, Pris quietly lifted Rusty by the arm. "Come on. Let's go back to the hotel."

Rusty brushed the sand from her knees. They walked arm in arm in silence as condemning thoughts tormented her mind. Pris let her fume.

Reaching the hotel, Pris asked quietly, "Did you and Carmen live at the brothel then?"

"No. Benny had told us to move out soon after Carmen became pregnant. He didn't want to send us away, but ‘having his best girl show up with a swollen stomach wouldn’t be good for business’, he said. He was kind and found us a nice place forty miles from his place by the lake, and a little over four hours south of Kansas City. It was quiet and discreet. Nobody knew us there, so it was all the better.”

“Did he come around much? You two were a couple in the day.”

“Not like I’d hoped. I thought he might move in with us. You know. Help out... be like family. But he distanced himself and stayed away. I didn’t see him until the day I... I tried to give the girl to him! But Benny didn’t want her either. Said she was damaged goods.”

“What?” shock filled Pris’s voice. “You tried to pawn Rosie off for the brothel? She’s not even a teenager yet.”

Rusty’s head bobbled as she nodded and shook her head at the same time. “He said no man wants a cripple. Said if I got rid of the kid, I could come back.”

Pris put her hand over her mouth at the news. She cleared her throat, and then asked, “Did you ever tell her about her father?”

“She was curious,” Rusty’s laugh was scornful. “But the first time she asked, I whipped her until she couldn’t stand up. Rosie learned to never question me again. I put the fear of God into her.”

"You should be ashamed, Rus'," Pris said, shaking her head Finally arriving back at the Chateau, they stopped outside the doors. "When was the last time you saw her?"

"Almost six months ago. The last thing I remember was seeing Rosie limp away towards the highway from my rearview mirror. She never looked back, and I never went to look for her. I was just glad to be done with her. I wanted Benny more."

Pris was at a loss for words, shaking her head in bewilderment. "So. What now, Rus'?"

"I've been thinking. Blacart's blasphemous show disgusted me last night, but something he said hit me. Something about your sins coming home to roost. My sins are many."

Pris nodded knowingly. "As are mine—"

"I can only hope there's not a day of accounting coming," said Rusty.

29 - THE LETTER

The desk clerk sniffed the air. Her nose picked up the rich cologne on the flamboyant preacher before he ever reached the reception desk. Looking up, she held out an envelope as he passed. “Reverend Blacart, a lady came and dropped this off for you.”

J.D. took the envelope, nodding his assent.

In his hotel suite, he laid the envelope on the table along with the offering bucket contents from the past night’s meeting. He changed into sweats and pulled a beer from the mini-frig. A sardonic smile crossed his lips as he sat down to count the stack of cash and checks. The Branson area had treated him kindly. The prayer cloths did especially well in this Bible-belt community. Pleased with the hefty amount, he put the money in his lockbox until he could get to the bank.

He shook his head at people’s ignorance. There was no such thing as a real miracle in his mind. So he made the miraculous happen. People everywhere believed whatever he said, and it made them happy. *And they pay me to do it!* His laugh was derisive.

He recalled a time many years before when a teenager, yelling and screaming, disrupted the meeting. He had passed her off as another lunatic wanting attention. Since then he'd learned better how to manipulate the masses.

Meetings were booked into the next year. After next summer, he would call it quits. Retire. Find a place on the Gulf where he could live the rest of his days in obscurity. It was time to put the show to rest before it got him into trouble.

Sinking back onto the chair, he picked up the sealed envelope staring him in the face. Big block letters printed in pen said *J.D. Blacart*. Figuring it was another thank-you letter or money, he slid his finger under the flap and opened it. Unfolding the yellow theme paper, he noted the lack of cash. First thought? Toss it into the waste can without reading it, but eager for more accolades, he settled back into the overstuffed armchair to decipher the scribbled writing.

"Jonathan Blacart

I was at your meeting last night. What a mockery. I knew two of the people you supposedly healed. Actors. Fakes. You're a phony, Blacart, and I intend to prove it. You're not a healer. You're a fraud. You have not fooled me. I know who you are.

Twelve years ago, you came to Benny's Place every night for a week to watch the girl with the gold scarf. Remember? Only you did a little more than eat and drink there, didn't you? Drunk with lust, you came back night after night until you followed the young underage girl up the stairs.

An involuntary shiver went through J.D.'s body. He sat up straight and searched his brain for places he'd been over a decade before –all the pubs, taverns, and brothels he'd visited. He'd had his share of women in his decrepit lifestyle. Yes, he hungered for the forbidden fruit–something to fill the empty void in his soul. If names described a person's character, then his name fit him well. Who was this girl with the gold scarf? He read on:

Her name was Carmen, and she was only 16. She was hooked by your charms. You devastated her. You dropped her like another pretty toy in your bag of tricks.

She searched for you over two years. When she found you in Eureka a couple of years later, I never saw her again. I don't know what you said or did, but this I know: YOU KILLED HER that night.

I'm holding you accountable. I will expose you for you who really are: a charlatan and a fraud.

Be ready.

No signature. *Who would write this?* J.D. shuddered

as snippets of old memories crept from the recesses of his mind. The stormy night in Eureka. The young girl toting a toddler on her hip stomping through the mud. Ranting and raving in the service. Shouting the child was his in front of the whole crowd. Proclaiming him to be a fraud. She had made such a commotion, the ushers had to grab the screaming baby from her arms, manhandle the girl, and push her outside the tent. When J.D. didn't hear anything more about her, he simply dismissed the whole thing and forgot about it. He reread parts of the letter again:

I don't know what you said or did, but YOU KILLED HER that night.

Now, with the letter shaking in his hand, J.D. put his head in his hands, the once-buried ten-year-old memory flooded his brain....

Yes. He remembered the beautiful red-haired glory–the tempting young vixen who entrapped him. There was no doubt. He remembered her young lithe body all over again, swooping, bending, beckoning to him as her silken red tresses fell like a crimson waterfall about her. Breathless. Yearning to touch. Sensual, forbidden thoughts replayed in his mind's eye. He recalled how the translucent fabric tightly hugged her breast and that gold scarf shimmered low upon her small hips. A seductive siren, she was. Untying the flimsy fabric, she had wafted its sweet smell of jasmine under his nose. Her sultry eyes entreated him to follow—and he did. It burned in his mind like live coals. His past had returned to haunt him.

YOU KILLED HER....

He wadded the letter into a tight ball.

You are a fraud!

He lit a match, setting the paper on fire.

... and I will expose you....

Tossing it into the wastebasket, he watched it burn. He was a devil who truly had a black heart, and he knew it. But he didn't care.

He only knew he had to get out of town. Fast.

30 – RETREAT

The last night–the biggest night of the whole week, and J.D. wasn't in the mood to perform. He wasn't foolish. Radical? Maybe. Impetuous? Sometimes. But he knew when a good run was over. It was time to leave the Branson area, even though the last meeting of the rally produced the biggest cash flow. His performance would be less than believable if he appeared tonight.

He made a call to one of the workers and then headed his motor home north toward Kansas, all the time thinking about the tent filling with people ready to witness another 'miracle.' He scoffed. Maybe a few extra days would clear his mind. More importantly, it would keep him at bay from the law. He had to keep moving before his scam was discovered.

People were still streaming into the tent from surrounding Branson areas even though the song service was almost finished. Everyone hoped to see the man who was said to have the magic touch, 'The Man with the Golden Hands.'

Rusty found her seat in the back with her friend Pris. She was determined to expose this man publicly before the whole congregation. Building up courage, her prepared speech was burning on the edge of her tongue. She planned to wait until the show started and then run up to the front pretending to be lame. He would have to work for it. When he prayed for her, she would refuse to be toppled by his hand and pretend to still be lame. Then, she'd call him out for what he was–a fake and a fraud. Screaming it from the top of her lungs, he'd be exposed for all to see that he was a deceiver and a liar. She played it out in her mind and waited, her restless leg tapping in anxiety.

People looked around for the famous preacher. Expecting him to run in from the back after the last song, everyone waited anxiously in the hot humid air. With no breeze to bring relief, minutes dragged by and workers appeared clueless for what to do. Agitation began to work throughout the crowd.

"What's going on?" asked one of the ushers. "Where's the preacher?"

"No idea," said the song leader. "It's unusual for him to be so late."

"Grand entrance?"

"Must have something planned we don't know about."

"Ask for testimonies. Something. Stall," suggested the usher. "Sing. Dance. Anything. People are getting antsy in this heat."

Workers tried to delay the service as long as possible, pulling back the big tent flaps, hoping for more air flow. Ladies fanned themselves frantically to get a little relief while men sat in sweaty agony waiting, checking their watches. Waiting. Waiting some more. Fans were turned toward the crowd, anything to settle the increasing anxiety.

Rusty shifted on the hard-wooden bench, rubbing her leg where it had gone to sleep. *Where IS he? He'd better show up.* A bead of sweat dripped from her face. *He won't get away with this sham.* As she dug out a tissue to wipe her brow, she saw an older man work his way to the front and whisper something into the song leader's ear.

The song leader grabbed a mike. "An emergency has come up and Reverend Blacart had to leave immediately to take care of family affairs. This will end tonight's service. Thank you all for coming and please make your last purchases at the front of the tent."

"What do you think—" Pris began.

"I think—" Rusty cut her off, "he's running."

Faith and Hope found their car at the edge of the cornfield-turned-into-a-parking lot.

"We drove all this way on the last night of meetings to hear J.D. Blacart and see him in action, and then he doesn't show," Faith said. "It was all for nothing."

"Word has it the last meeting of the week is always the most spectacular," said Hope.

"I wanted to bring Rosie with us," said Faith, "so maybe her leg could be healed."

"Not the right time, sis. At least we got a couple of prayer cloths."

"Must have been some crisis in his family for him to cancel the last meeting."

"My, yes. We must pray for him. He might need a miracle of his own tonight."

"That we can do, sister."

They drove a few miles down the road in silence until Hope spoke. "It's been over six months now, hasn't it?"

"Six months since what?" Faith glanced over, as she turned onto their corner.

"Since we first met our Rosie."

"She certainly has come out of her quiet, shy little shell we found her in," commented Faith.

Hope laughed out loud. "She isn't the shy one anymore. That's what God's love can do."

"Did CPS ever find anything more about Nina?".

"We would be the last to know," said Hope, "but I think not. Otherwise, wouldn't Rosie be headed back to live with her?"

Faith parked the car in the garage. "Not necessarily. If Nina isn't fit to care for Rosie, then

Rosie could be eligible for adoption."

"I know God works things out for good to those who believe," Hope said as they entered their little home. "So, He'll work it out for Rosie too."

31 – ADVICE

"What did you mean, Rusty, when you said, 'he's running?'" Pris asked, as she opened the driver's door of her Lexus.

Rusty got in the passenger side. "J.D.'s running from trouble." She gave her friend a knowing look. "I told him I was going to expose him." Rusty's laugh was raw. "He skipped town before I could pull it off."

"And how did you think you'd do that?" Pris flipped the blinker to turn left onto the highway toward Benny's.

"By proving he was a phony. I was going to get in his healing line and pretend, just like you. Only I wasn't going to play along. I planned to call him out in front of everyone."

"Oh... Rusty..." Pris shook her head in slow motion as she glanced over toward her friend. Her voice held a touch of fear. "You don't know Jon Blacart. He could talk his way out of any dung hole and come out looking spit clean."

"Ha! I know him better than you think. Why do think he ran? Something spooked him, and I think it was my letter. He knows what he did." She spat the words.

Pris cringed at the fury in Rusty's voice. "You're bound and determined, aren't you?"

"You bet I am. He killed my Carmie. I vow to make him admit it."

"There's a burger place up ahead. Want to get a bite?" Pris hoped to calm Rusty's vengeance for the moment.

"Yeah, sure. Why not?"

They parked, went in, and found a booth. After ordering, Rusty kept up the rampage. "Where's he going next? You should know. You said you follow his circuit."

"Right now? I don't know. He'll be traveling all the way up to Kansas City and eventually work his way back down hitting towns here and there all the way to Texas. That's been his routine. But again," Pris hedged. "He may go farther north. Who am I to know?"

"When will he be in *this* area again?"

Their food arrived, and Pris waited until they were alone again. "Oh, Rusty. Really, you don't want—"

"Come on," Rusty urged with an edge to her voice. "I know you know." The silence grew strained. She chomped a bite and stared down her nose at her friend. The fire in Rusty's eyes burned, "You owe it to me, Pris."

Pris wiped her mouth slowly with a napkin to stall. “Well, I can try to find out. That’s the best I can do.”

“Pris,” Rusty’s volume rose. She took a gulp of her soda. “You can do better than that.”

Pris crinkled her forehead and pushed her platinum-blond hair behind her ear. “Okay, okay. Uh... some time next summer.”

Rusty pursed her lips, placated for the moment. “I can wait.” Her eyes narrowed. She pinched her lips together. “I can wait.”

Pris remained quiet and finished her sandwich. Rusty took one last sip of her soda and then pushed away her plate of uneaten food as she brooded.

“Ready to go?” asked Pris as she took a last gulp of water.

“Yeah, I guess.”

They drove the rest of the way to Benny’s Place in silence. Parking the car, Pris turned to her friend. “Before you get out, I have to ask you a serious question. Have you, uh...” she paused, “have you given any more thought to Rosie?”

Rusty’s breath came out in a huff. She closed her eyes in a crinkled frown. “For ten years, she’s been the dirt under my feet; an anchor holding me down.”

“Just because she’s J.D.’s kid?”

“She’s the devil’s seed,” she spat with emphasis.

Pris bit the inside of her cheek at the harsh

declaration. "But she is also Carmie's daughter—"

"No. She's HIS daughter. Every time I looked at Rosie, all I could see was him." Rusty began to open the car door.

Pris grabbed for Rusty's arm. "She is still a part of Carmie."

Rusty closed the door and turned to face her friend. "You've got to understand. Whatever I've done to Rosie was because she had to know life was tough. I showed her the world would not be fair or kind to a cripple."

"All because life dealt *you* a harsh blow?"

"I wasn't about to show her any love that would make her soft."

"...but she is only a child."

Rusty heaved her shoulders. "Come on, Pris. Let's talk inside."

The pub was crowded for 11:00 p.m. Rusty and Pris found their way to a back table and sat. The waitress brought them water and menus.

"We're not ordering," Rusty's manner was abrupt and rude. Her expression held scorn and bitterness as she waited for them to be alone. "First, I blamed the preacher," she snorted. "And then...I blamed God." She put her hands on her head. "But it wasn't God's fault," her voice lowered to a whisper. "It was mine." She quieted at the realization.

"How do you mean?"

"You know the words of the Lord's Prayer?"

Pris seemed puzzled.

"The part that says, '*Lead us not into temptation....*' I blamed God. The temptation was everywhere: Benny, the other guys, the brothel, the lifestyle..." Rusty groaned. "But it wasn't them. It was me. I blamed God for leading me into temptation, for leading Carmie into temptation, but I walked right into it all by myself and *became* the temptation." She pounded a closed fist to her chest.

"You worked your charm back in the day, I'll admit that. That's why Benny loved you." Pris said.

Rusty scoffed. "He loved the business I brought in, you mean. Then I...." She stopped and frowned at the ceiling as the memory re-emerged. "I led my own daughter into temptation and showed her how to work it. And Benny loved me even more."

"You did a good job of that," Pris admitted. "You're a mess, Rus. Go get a good night's sleep. Tomorrow I'm going back to Texas. I'll call you before I leave for home."

The following morning, Pris called. "Calling to say goodbye, but I wondered. Where do you think Rosie went? I'm worried about her."

"How would I know? I didn't care when she left,

and I don't care now."

Pris ignored her indifference. "Do you think someone picked her up?"

"Like the kind of men who come through Benny's?" The tough interior of Rusty Delahunt's heart hardened even more. "At least then she'd have a warm bed with someone."

"Rusty! I can't believe how cruel and hard-hearted you've become. Your soul must be as cold as iron. This girl is your own flesh and blood, for heaven's sake. She's your *granddaughter,* and someday she may come back home. You need to be there in case she does."

"I really hope she doesn't. I have my own life to worry about." Rusty picked at the polish on her chipped nails. She frowned. "What if the police catch up with me?"

"You'll have to take your chances on that one. I'm telling you–leave Benny. He's no good for you. Go home. Do something right for once. You didn't want to be a grandmother twelve years ago, but you became one. And you're *still* Rosie's grandmother. It's time for you to act like one."

Rusty twitched. "Ha. I'm no grandmother–never have been." The woman grunted. "Rosie's been gone over six months. She may never be found."

Pris threw her hands up in the air with

exasperation. "So, call the police if you're all of a sudden so concerned."

Rusty exhaled deeply. "Never. You know I can't call them. Benny told me someone from the Queen City police had already been snooping around my place. No, I won't call them."

"It's doubtful then that they'll return. Go home– Go back to Abbotsville."

Silence on Rusty's end of the line.

"Say something, Rus'."

Heavy breathing. A long pause....

"Goodbye, Pris."

32 - CALL FROM HAZEL

Detective Flanders had no sooner stepped into his office when his phone rang.

"Mr. Flanders?" asked the voice on the other end.

"Speaking."

"This is Hazel. Hazel Walters. Remember me? From over in Abbotsville? You told me to call if I had any more information."

"What do you have for me, Hazel?" He tried to sound congenial.

"Well, sir." She took a tone of importance, "Rusty is back home."

Flanders's heart quickened. "Are you sure?"

"I saw her get out of her car and go inside. Yes, sir. I know her car, and it was her."

"Do you know when she got there?"

"A few hours ago, I believe. The car wasn't there this morning when I went out to get my mail, but after lunch I saw it."

"Is she alone?"

"Think so. Didn't see anyone with her."

"Do me a favor, Hazel?" He put some sugar in his voice.

"Sure, Detective. Anything you want."

“Don’t tell anyone else–especially Rusty–about calling me.”

“Are you going undercover, Detective?” She whispered into her phone.

“Let’s just say it’s our little secret, okay?” He kept his voice mysterious.

Flanders clicked off his phone, elated with the news. Rusty Delahunt had finally been found. He hoped she would stay put until he or Ms. Anders could talk to her. He immediately called to tell her.

Ms. Anders listened to Flanders’s news with casual disinterest. “I tried calling the number you gave me for Rusty, but it had been disconnected. But I’m way ahead of you on Rusty being home.” Ms. Anders sounded smug. “A lady named Priscilla Connery called the Queen City police with a tip saying Rusty was headed back home. They called me. They gave me Rusty’s unlisted phone number. I was just about to call her.”

“Interesting. Do think Rosie will ever be placed back with her grandmother?”

“It depends on what Rusty tells me and what I see at the home. I’ll need to do a written assessment.”

“Well, keep me posted, will you? I need to know whether to bring the cuffs or not.”

It brought a chuckle to Ms. Anders. “I know you’re half joking, Detective, but of course, I’ll keep you in the loop."

Hanging up from the detective, Ms. Anders punched in Rusty's number. "Good afternoon. Rusty Delahunt?"

"Yeah. Who's this?" came Rusty's gruff voice.

"My name is Stacey Anders. I'm with Child Protective Services in Ridgetown."

Silence. Rusty's heart pounded so loud she was sure it could be heard.

"Ms. Delahunt, are you there?"

Rusty cleared her suddenly tightened throat. "Uh.... yah."

"I'll be direct, Ms. Delahunt. We have your granddaughter, Rose."

Rusty choked. "How did you get my number?"

"We have our connections. Rose is fine, in case you want to know." Ms. Anders's voice reflected sarcasm. "However," Anders paused for effect, "I have questions. When is the best time for me to come for a visit?"

Rusty gulped and a coughed on her spit. "Uh...."

"You *do* plan on staying in the area for a while, don't you?"

"Uh...." Long pause.

"You would not be wise to run again," Ms. Anders warned.

The resignation was evident. "I'm done running."

Rusty blew out her breath slowly.

"Good. Then tomorrow at 2:00 p.m.? I'll come to your place."

This time the woman sounded defeated. Caught. "I'll be here," she squeaked.

33 - THE TALK

The supervisor found Rosie and Kim watching television in the activity room. "Ms. Anders is here to see you, Rose. Please go to the office."

Rosie's fears always went up a notch or two whenever she heard her caseworker's name. *She wouldn't come just to visit, so what does she want?* She limped to the office with a neatly tied worry knot in her stomach.

"Rose! Come in!" Ms. Anders gave her a pleasant smile. "You look well. Please sit." She pointed to a chair opposite her.

The girl tried to smile and sat down with suspicion on her mind.

"I've heard about you here at the Home," Ms. Anders said. "You're learning to play the piano?"

Rosie blushed in spite herself. "I love to play," she said simply.

"I'd love to hear you play sometime, but it's not why I came today."

Here it comes. Have faith. She felt her body stiffen as she braced for bad news.

"We found your grandmother. She's back home in

Abbotsville. I thought you'd want to know."

Rosie's face went pale as her body recoiled. Rosie's eyes widened. "Pleee-ase, don't send me back. She kicked me out. Warned me to never come back." She clutched the edge of her chair with tight fists.

"Maybe she wants you back? Changed her mind?"

"No! She hates me. Doesn't want me." Rosie hung her head.

"She said that to you, Rose?"

Rosie nodded.

"I didn't mean to alarm you. I'm sorry. In any case, I must talk to your grandmother first. Then we can determine if you go back to her or not."

Rosie relaxed a bit.

"In the meantime, you'll continue to stay here at the Children's Home."

Rosie went to the music room early the next day for her weekly piano lesson. Pounding on the keys helped to release her frustration. She sat down and began to play impromptu, beating out the stress and anxieties. As she closed her eyes and let her fingers discover the keys, a sad melancholy tune emerged through the piano strings. Then, in a deep crescendo, a majestic melody of praise, sweet and pure, arose as new life sprung from death. It was like God seemed to play His melody through her fingers.

Hope stood in the doorway and treasured the girl's God-given gift. Her eyes brimmed. "Praise be...Oh, my sweet Rosie," Hope expressed in awe. "What wonderful, glorious praise! The sweetest I've ever heard. I'm captivated with your music. What a marvelous gift God's given you."

"Hope!" Rosie slid off the piano bench to wrap her arms around her piano teacher and friend. "I'm so glad you're here. I need to talk to you. Ms. Anders wants to send me back to Nina." She choked on the words. "I don't know if.... I can't go back... I...I...just...can't."

Hope wrinkled her brow. "Oh, sweetie, I hadn't heard."

"Can you do something? Talk to Ms. Anders?"

"I'm not sure my words would mean anything to her, sweetie. But there is something much more powerful I can do, and you can too." She stroked the girl's arm.

Rosie looked puzzled.

"Pray, child. The most powerful weapon anyone has. Remember when I said God can make a way when there seems to be no way? He is always working things out for your good, even when you can't see it happening. He works behind the scenes and is *always* doing something." She gave Rosie another hug. "So, sweetie, what do I always tell you?"

"Hold on to faith." Rosie blinked away the tears.

"With everything you have. Yes. What else?"

"Have hope."

"Hmmm..." Hope smiled with approval. "And that's why it's called faith. You can be sure that everything you hope for will either happen or something better will come to be, even when you can't see it. He may even have something better than you can imagine. And then our God of hope can fill you with all joy and peace in your heart. Do you believe that?"

She wiped her face and then grabbed Hope's arm. "Without you or Faith, I wouldn't have any hope–or faith."

"Tonight, before you go to bed, read the eleventh chapter of Hebrews, okay?"

That evening after Rosie donned her PJs, she got out her treasured Bible and curled up on her bed.

"Reading that old book again, Goody-Two-Shoes?"

"It's got a lot to say, Kim. You should read it sometime," she said. On impulse, she decided to jab back. "Or can't you read?"

The astonished look on Kim's face revealed her weakness. "Who told?"

That feeling of inner satisfaction felt good. "Maybe God told on you." She grinned.

"Well, I can read a little," Kim said in defense, "but not real good."

"Come sit by me and I'll read it to you."

With all the punch knocked out of her, Kim meekly came over and joined Rosie on her bed. With hunched shoulders, she sat and listened as Rosie read God's Word and watched in curiosity as Rosie bowed her head prayed out loud.

"God, please help Kim, and help me with Nina. I'm scared. But I'm gonna trust you to take care of me."

34 – ASSESSMENT

Rusty was ready for Stacey Anders's visit. She had cleaned the house and prepared herself mentally. Observing herself in the mirror, she halfway approved. *The sweater and pants combo make me look a little younger, but nothing will cover these wrinkles.* She reapplied her lipstick and dabbed concealer over the old scar by her hairline. Finger-brushing bangs over her forehead, she assured the mark her dad once gave her was covered. *Life has not been merciful to me.* She released a huge sigh.

The caseworker promptly arrived at 2:00 p.m.

"Come in, Ms.—" Rusty eyed the young woman in her crisp navy-blue pantsuit.

"Stacey Anders."

Ms. Anders entered Rusty's home and did a quick overview with her eyes. Her three-inch stilettos clicked over to the couch where she took a seat. Snapping open her leather briefcase, she pulled out a few papers, and then looked Rusty in the eye. "I will be recording our conversation if you don't mind."

Rusty sat on the edge of a cushioned chair across from her. "You can call me Rusty."

Ms. Anders clicked the recorder to the 'on' position

and then faced Rusty. "You said your name is Rusty Delahunt. But in truth your given name is really Rozlyn Gavotte. Correct?"

Rusty's eyes got large, her voice defensive. "Uh...Delahunt is my maiden name. I took it back after the divorce. Rusty is only a nickname I've gone by since my high school days."

"Yes. I know." Ms. Anders was quick to reply. "All well and good. But I need to hear you speak it. In fact, I know a lot about you. Some facts must be verified for the record. Other questions must be answered. That's the reason I'm here, and, of course, on behalf of Rose's welfare."

Rusty scowled at the mention of Rosie's name. She folded her arms across her chest and sat back in her chair. Ms. Anders give her a queer look and then wrote something in her notebook.

"Okay. Easy questions first. What is your relationship to Rose? Aunt? Grandmother? Guardian?"

"My daughter, Carmen, was her mother."

"Grandmother, then. I understand her mother is deceased. How long has Rose lived with you?"

"Since she was two and one-half years old."

"And how long was that?"

"Ten years. She will be thirteen this September."

"More like twelve years, then. She's been in this

home since her birth, correct?"

Rusty's mouth dropped open but she did not speak, only nodded.

"Did the court award you a guardianship?"

Ms. Anders was met with a blank stare.

"Legal custody. Were you given legal custody of Rose?"

Still the blank stare.

"Okay. I'll take that as a no. Did you ever receive state assistance or compensation?"

"No. I took care of Rosie on my own."

"Did you? Really? I heard a man named Benny helped you out."

Rusty's eyebrows lifted at Benny's name. "You called him too?"

"I have my sources. I told you I know quite a bit already."

Her shoulders sagged. "Yes," she sighed, "Benny paid the rent."

"Good. Do you work?"

"Uh..." her face scrunched into a scowl. "I have gainful employment." She picked at her nails.

"Where are you employed?" the caseworker pressed.

"Uh...Benny's Place."

"Okay," Ms. Anders wrote another note on her pad and placed a big check mark by it.

Rusty arose from her seat and paced to the window. Looking out, she saw her neighbor, Hazel, peering from her front window. *Old biddy. Never minds her own business.* She shook her head in disgust.

"Where did Rose go to school?"

Rusty cleared her throat. "I, uh…well… you could say I homeschooled her. The girl was a slow learner. Listen, Ms. Anders, are we about finished?"

"No–" Ms. Anders was firm. "We have a lot to cover yet. This may take a while." She crossed her legs and flipped to a new page of her notebook.

"Then would you mind if I made coffee? My nerves are in jitters."

"Sure–only if you promise not to duck out the back door."

"Come watch me if you must, but I got to get some coffee."

Ms. Anders rose from the couch and followed Rusty into the kitchen, taking her recorder with her. She sat at the kitchen table and continued. "Now. The tough questions. If Rose was a slow learner like you said, how did you motivate her?"

Rusty put three heaping tablespoons of coffee into the coffeepot and set it to brew. *How can I put this?*

"Ms. Delahunt?"

"I…uh…I made her learn."

"How, exactly?" Ms. Anders pressed.

Rusty thought long and hard. *I can't tell her about the whippings I gave her. I can't say I slapped her so silly she passed out. I can't tell her....* Her body trembled with an involuntary shiver. Her reddened face broke out in perspiration. She swiped at it with her arm and after a few seconds, formulated an answer. "I made her tough. After all, the world is not kind to a cripple. She had to learn, and I did not let her slack."

"You're saying you disciplined her, then?" Anders added more notes to her pad.

"You bet I did." Rusty felt good with that answer, thinking it was the right one.

Ms. Anders studied her notes, wrote some more, and then was silent so long it worried Rusty. As she poured herself a cup of coffee, her shaky hand almost spilled it all over the counter. She sat down and held tightly onto her cup to stop her hand from trembling.

Ms. Anders focused on the woman's face. "Rusty, did you abandon Rose?"

That one caught her off-guard. Rusty stared into the hot black liquid. No answer.

"Rose said you kicked her out. Is that true?"

No answer. No eye contact. Rusty drew an invisible circle on the table.

"Did she run away?"

"No. She didn't run away," Rusty's voice came out in gravelly hoarseness.

"Rusty," Ms. Anders' voice became firmer, a little louder. "Did you tell her to leave?"

Rusty gritted her teeth. She cocked her head in defense. "I might have said some mean things to the girl."

"You mean, your granddaughter."

Rusty scowled. Her nervous leg kept bobbing up and down.

"I need verbal responses, Rusty. Rosie said you didn't want her. Said you don't love her anymore. True?"

Pour on the waterworks, Rusty. She forced tears to her eyes. "I didn't mean it. Really, I'm not a bad person." She made her voice quiver.

Ms. Anders did not seem moved. She scribbled more notes. "We're almost finished for today. This ends the written part. May I see Rose's room?"

Rusty quickly rose from her chair, glad for the questioning to be done. "S-s-sure," she stammered. "But there's nothing to find. She took everything she owns."

Ms. Anders was shown the small bedroom. She flipped on the light switch which was outside of the closet. What she saw inside made her catch her breath. The crayon markings on the wall the detective had seen appeared to count days. Ants crawled on some dried crumbs laying on the floor. An empty coffee can that smelled of urine sat in the corner. After taking photos with her phone, Ms. Anders took a deep breath, put on her game face, and met Rusty back in the living room.

"Thank you for your time, Rusty. I have one more question. Please, take your time to answer." She waited for Rusty to acknowledge the seriousness of her voice and look her in the eye.

Rusty nodded with a question on her face. "What else is there?"

"Are you aware of all the trouble you may be in?"

Ms. Anders was met with a blank stare from the woman who hated Rosie.

35 - COURT ORDER

Ms. Anders finished her formal written assessment of Rusty Delahunt and her home and presented it to the court. Rusty had agreed to go to counseling in accordance with a plea deal.

A couple of weeks later, she met with Rosie again.

"Please, Ms. Anders, you can't make me go!" Rosie pleaded. "I don't ever want to go back there."

Ms. Anders watched the terror return to Rosie's eyes—the same fear she had seen the day she picked the girl up from the Abrams' home: her body tense, fists clenched, anxiety high. Her distress was real.

"Your Nina has been to counseling ordered by the court. She asked if she could see you once more before—" Ms. Anders didn't finish when Rosie spurted out.

"But Nina HATES me!" Surprised at her own outburst, she hung her head. "And I'm... I'm afraid."

"Rose," Ms. Anders said in a quiet voice. "Did Nina ever hit you?"

Her face said it all.

Ms. Anders dared to take a stab in the dark. "Did

she ever lock you in your closet?" she whispered.

Rosie gave her a 'how-did-you-know' look with widened eyes. She clasped her hand over her mouth lest she divulge the dirty secret. "I hate that dark hidey hole."

"I saw your closet, Rose. I only guessed. Why would she put you there?"

Rosie hung her head in shame. "Lots of things. It was always my fault."

"No, it was never your fault." Ms. Anders put her hand over the top of Rosie's.

Rosie shook her head. "Said she was putting the fear of God into me but it only made me afraid of her." The words tumbled out before she could stop them.

"She wants to talk to you. Maybe she's changed."

Rosie shook her head again. "No. I don't believe it."

"She said she'll only talk to you. The judge agreed to let your grandmother see you if she cooperated with us. We will bring her here so you will be in a safe place, and I'll be there right beside you."

Rosie felt a deep sadness as she left, head hanging low. She wished Hope could come to talk to her, but she would have to wait until next piano lesson.

The following week, Rosie unloaded her soul. Her piano lessons had become her link to God. "Hope, what am I going to do? The judge said I have to see

Nina. Ms. Anders will be there too, but I'm still scared."

"If the judge ordered it, then you'll have to go, but it's good to know Ms. Anders will be there with you the whole time. She'll protect you. And more importantly, you'll have God there with you, too."

"But what will I say?" Rose bit at her nails.

"You may not need to say much at all. Just be honest. Tell Ms. Anders what you fear and what you feel. Your safety is her utmost concern. She'll watch for danger signs."

"But... but what if she makes me go back? What if..."

"What if's may never be, child. Right now, all you need to think about is having a conversation. And what else do you need to do?"

"Hold on to faith." Rosie rolled her eyes.

"And what do you need to have?"

"Hope."

"Hope is a powerful force, and faith will bring you through it all. Did you know Jesus is standing at the right hand of His Father right now praying for you?"

"Really?" Rosie's eyes got big with wonder.

"That's right. And He's praying your faith won't fail. He cares about you, honey. Remember? God is working even when you can't see it. You must learn to trust the wait."

"Hope?"

"Yes, Rosie?"

"You're the best friend I ever had." She threw her small arms around the large woman.

"And I'll always be there for you, child," Hope laughed out loud and squeezed her in return.

36 - DREADED DAY

The dreaded day arrived, and Ms. Anders drove over to the Children's Home to pick up Rosie. Rosie's hand shook so much she couldn't open the car door. Ms. Anders opened it, assuring the girl she'd be with her the whole time. Terrible memories plagued her from the last day she spent with Nina.

"Your grandmother will only talk to you today," Ms. Anders said as they drove. "The visit will be short. She will have time to say what she wants, and then you can ask questions or say whatever you want—if you wish. You don't have to say anything if you don't want to. Remember, I will be right beside you the whole time."

"Yes, Ms. Anders." She picked at her fingers and stared out the car window.

"If you feel uncomfortable or unsafe at any time or want to leave, all you need to do is say so. I won't let anything happen to you."

"Okay," she mouthed. The word didn't come out. A shiver made her pull her sweater more tightly around her.

Rusty was directed to the appointed room in the county office and sat waiting with a magazine in her lap, bobbing her knee up and down.

When Rosie entered the room with Ms. Anders, Rusty quickly hopped to her feet and rushed to Rosie with outstretched arms. Rosie shied behind the social worker like a skittish colt. *Nina never smiled at me before… and never wanted to hug me.*

"It's okay, Rose. I'm here." Ms. Anders leaned down and whispered.

Rusty grabbed at Rosie's hand, pulling her from behind Ms. Anders. "I'm glad you came to see me."

Her reflexes kicked in and she pulled her hand back. Breathing quickened as she stared at the floor. When Rusty touched her finger on the jagged scar, Rosie stiffened and reared back with a shiver. *I didn't want to; they MADE me.* Rosie's large black eyes looked to Ms. Anders for reassurance.

Ms. Anders quickly stepped in front of the girl to shield her from the woman. "You sit over there, Ms. Delahunt." She pointed to the other side of the table. "Rosie and I will sit over here."

Rusty huffed, stomped around the long conference table, yanked out a chair, and then seated herself. She glared at her granddaughter across the table and held her hands together.

Ms. Anders stroked Rosie's back, and then pulled out chairs for them. Seating herself, she clicked on the recorder. "This will be a short meeting today, Ms.

Delahunt. You begin."

Rusty shifted uneasily in the hard, wooden chair and used the sweet voice Rosie had heard at Benny's. "Rosie, I was sooo worried about you."

Rosie squinted at her grandmother, holding her mouth in a thin line. *Yeah, right. I heard that sickening voice when you talked to Benny. I'm not gonna believe a word you say.*

"I'm sorry for the pain I caused you, honey."

Rosie glared at her. *She's never called me honey. And she's NOT sorry. She's lying.* She shook her head slowly in disbelief.

"I'm trying to change. Things will be different. You'll see."

Rosie tightened her lips as she stared at a coffee cup ring on the table.

"I didn't mean what I did and said."

Rosie narrowed her eyes at her grandmother. *Nina's only pretending to be nice because Ms. Anders is here. She faked being nice before when it suited her. She's a liar.*

"Will you forgive me?"

The knot in Rosie's belly twisted at the unbelievable request. A frown creased her forehead as she kept her head down. She raised her chin in sudden defiance with a new boldness. She lifted her eyes toward Ms. Anders for reassurance and then without a blink, she kept her voice firm but quiet. "No, Nina."

Rusty's behavior took an ominous turn. She shoved her chair back with a screech and stood. The cords of her neck became taut; her lips pursed. Rosie felt those darkened mascaraed eyes burning a hole right through her.

"What do you mean... *NO*?" Rusty's voice raised a notch through gritted teeth. "You dare to defy me, girl?" Her hand smacked the table so hard in front of Rosie it made her jump.

She cowered for a moment and then remembered Ms. Anders's words. Rosie turned to face Ms. Anders and raised herself from the chair. "Ms. Anders? I want to leave. Now? Please?"

Ms. Anders nodded, stood and gathered her papers together. "We're done for today, Ms. Delahunt. It was quite revealing." She gave Rusty a stern look as they passed her, leaving her fuming in a huff with a face looking like it would explode.

On the way back to the Children's Home, Rosie stared out the window. Her hands still shook as she tried to hold them still in her lap. Her mind was in turmoil. *Hold on to faith. God's working, Hope said. But how? But I'll be strong–because I'm trusting in God. I just hope I don't have to go back and live with Nina.*

"What happens now, Ms. Anders?"

"In many cases, children are reunited with their parents or their closest relative. In your case, your grandmother—."

"You won't make me go back to her, will you?" Rosie turned to look at her, her fingernails going into her mouth.

"After today's visit, I think it's better that you stay in protective custody."

"Whew." She breathed a sigh of relief. "I'm glad. What about Nina?"

"Your grandmother is in big trouble. I don't believe much of what she said today, do you?"

"No. She was lying–like always."

"She's going to counseling and will still have to appear in court for several things. She may even have to go to jail for what she's done."

"Will I have to see her again?"

"Your Nina is working with us on other matters, so the court was lenient in permitting this visit today. There won't be any other visits unless you request it, and then we'll have to decide if it's in your best interests."

"So then I can stay at the Children's Home?" She put her hands together in prayer form in unspoken thanks as a smile broke out on her face.

"For now, yes. It's the best place for you until I can find a suitable match for foster care."

"Oh." Rosie's hope faded as quick as it rose. Another worry to pray about.

37 – EMERGENCY

"I've found you a foster home," Ms. Anders told Rosie a few weeks after the visitation. "Your foster parents are eager to meet you."

Rosie's body tensed. She thought of the horror stories the other kids shared about their foster families. *Were these good people?* "But you said I could stay at the Children's Home."

"Yes—until I found you a good foster family. It's best for you to be in a family setting," said Ms. Anders. "You don't have to worry. They are good people. I'll take you to their house next Monday and introduce you."

When Hope entered the music room, she found Rosie bent over the keys with her head in her hands. As Hope scooted in beside Rosie on the piano bench, Hope's face broke out in a sweat.

"Oh, my. What a dizzy spell." Hope began to frantically fan herself. "And it's not even that hot out today." A weak chuckle escaped her lips. "Now, what's wrong, darling? Are you okay? Are you sick?"

"Oh, Hope. I'm just sad. This is the last time I'll see

you."

"What? Why? Where's this coming from, Rosie?"

"I'm being moved next week." A deep breath escaped her lips.

"Where?"

"To a foster home."

"In Ridgetown?"

"I don't know. I wasn't told. I don't even know their names. I'm afraid, Hope. What if they're bad people like some other kids have talked about? What if they don't like me? What if...?"

Hope wagged her index finger. "What have I told you about worrying over 'what if's'?"

Rosie rolled her eyes. "They may never become 'what-ares'. I know. But I'm still really nervous."

"Well, prethous girl, it's perfectly nashural to be nervoush." Hope's words slurred. "Le's pray God worksh—" Hope gasped and grabbed her chest.

"Hope! What is it? What's wrong?"

Hope's eyes looked desperate. "My... my heart... I c-c-can't..." the plump lady leaned on Rosie. Her face flushed a bright red.

"Please, Hope. Sit up. HELP! Somebody, HELP!" Rosie yelled and then realized the door to the soundproof piano room was closed.

Hope's breaths came in short gasps. "I'm... so... so... dizsh..y...." Her body slumped over the keys making them clang before she passed out.

Rosie pushed the older lady off her arm and hurried to go to help. She fell to her knees on the floor as she slipped off the piano bench. "HELP!" she yelled. Picking herself up, she stumbled on her own feet as she tried to run. At the door, her heart fell when she remembered the offices were on the upper floors. *Oh no! I'll never make it.* She punched the Main Level button in the elevator. *COME ON! COME ON!* Punch. Punch. Punch. *HURRY!*

Rosie watched as the ambulance drove away with Hope inside. Sick with worry, she barely slept the whole weekend. "Hope has to be okay, God. Please.... Don't let anything happen to my best friend," she prayed. And then Hope's words echoed in her mind: *Keep the faith. Have hope, and trust the wait.*

Her soul in anguish, her heart filled with worry and fear.

38 - FOSTER PARENTS

The following Monday, Rosie put her belongings into the back seat and got into the car with Ms. Anders.

“Ms. Anders, have you heard anything about Hope? Is she okay?”

“Hope Abrams? Your piano teacher?”

Rosie went on to tell her about Hope’s incident the few days before and how scared she was when the ambulance came and took her away. “I hope she’s okay. Thought I’d never get to the office.”

“I can check on her for you. I’m sure she’ll be fine, Rose.” Wanting to turn Rosie’s mind another direction, Ms. Anders changed the subject. “By the way, I think you’ll really like your foster parents. They don’t have any children and live in a nice neighborhood. Good people.”

Rosie twisted her hands, overcome with new emotions. *Just me? All alone with strange people?*

“Will I be there forever?”

“Oh, no. It’s only temporary for now.”

“Oh.” She hoped these people would treat her nice and not be mean and hateful like Nina. Then more frightening thoughts entered her mind. *What if they’re like Maddie's foster parents who didn't feed her? Or like Kim's mean parents? What if...?*

"You're very quiet, Rose." Ms. Anders noted. "Deep in thought?"

Rosie nodded. "Thinking about the what ifs and what ares."

"That's very interesting."

"Yeah. Something Hope used to tell me."

"You really like Hope, don't you?"

"She's my best friend—my only friend. Without her, I'd be—" She thought a minute. "Well, I don't know where I'd be–but really without hope."

"Don't worry. Everything will work out."

For my good? I can only hope and pray.

Driving west of Ridgetown toward Shepherd's Creek Road, Rosie recognized the Dairy Queen where Hope and Faith once took her for ice cream. They passed Walmart and a few other landmarks. Sitting up straight to get a better look out the windshield, she felt her eyes pop when Ms. Anders parked the car by the curb beside Shepherd's Creek Assembly. Rosie got out and followed Ms. Anders to the house adjacent to the church.

Mary Davis saw them coming and opened the door. "Jim, they're here," she called down the basement stairs. Turning back toward the caseworker and the girl, she smiled warmly. "You must be Rose.

Please come in. We've been waiting for you. Your room is ready!"

Rosie relaxed and smiled back. *She seems nice. Pretty, too.*

Jim Davis came up the stairs from his study and was astonished when he saw them. "Rosie?"

"Pastor Jim?" Rosie gave Ms. Anders a questioning look. "Pastor Jim and his wife are my foster parents?" Excitement lit up her eyes and a huge grin spread across her face.

"You already know each other?" Ms. Anders was likewise amazed.

Jim Davis was all smiles. "Yes, we've known each other for a while now. We met at church."

"I hope it doesn't present a problem," Ms. Anders said.

"No problem at all," Rosie grinned throwing her arms around Pastor Jim's waist.

"No problem at all," Pastor Jim agreed.

39 - THE SURGEON'S REPORT

A few weeks passed and Rosie easily felt at home with the Davises. She had asked several times about Hope, but never heard what she wanted to hear – that Hope was going to be okay. Mary had taken over as pianist in the church services, but everyone missed Hope's playing and jovial personality.

"Hope is recuperating in the hospital after her heart attack," explained Mary.

"I wish I could see her," wished Rose out loud.

"She's too weak. It's taking all her strength to get better. Faith and Pastor Jim are the only ones allowed to visit. You can pray for her, though."

"You sound like Hope," said Rosie, "she was always telling me to pray, have hope, and keep the faith."

"She's a good godly woman."

One day, while Pastor Jim and his wife were chatting about the day over coffee, he spoke out of the blue. "I wish we could do something for Rosie's leg. It pains me to see her grimace every time her foot turns sideways."

"I know. Even walking is hard for her. Perhaps we

should take her to an orthopedic surgeon and see what he says."

"Make the call, Mary. I agree."

The Davises found a well-known orthopedic surgeon and had Rosie's leg x-rayed again. They informed him of Dr. Mark Edwards's examination a few months before. The doctor said he would corroborate his findings with the other doctor. A few days later, the couple received a call for a private consultation.

"Here is what I found, Mr. and Mrs. Davis. Almost all the bones in her leg had been crushed, and the growth plate was damaged when it was most vulnerable. That's why the leg grew a bit shorter than the other. It is no wonder she limps."

The Davises gave each other a somber look. "We were so hopeful—" Mary began.

"How did it happen?" Jim asked.

"Dr. Edwards found the intake summary from when Rosie was life-flighted to the hospital; she was around two years old. When paramedics arrived at the scene of the car accident, Rosie was still in her car seat. Her little leg was crushed between the car seat and the smashed-in car door. The mother lived for a few months, but she was in a coma until she died."

"That is truly sad," said Mary. "Is there any possible hope for Rosie's leg?"

"No. I'm so sorry. Rosie's leg is irreparable. If she would have had an operation when she was younger, there may have been more expectations. It doesn't appear anything was done. The leg has grown this way for too long."

"And her face? Did she get that gash in the same accident?"

"Broken glass from the windshield barely missed her jugular vein. Again, plastic surgery could have fixed the three-inch scar. Any closer, and she would have lost her vision in that eye but it appears there were no other doctor visits."

Mary gasped. "Poor child. It's a miracle Rosie is alive."

Saddened at the news, Jim and Mary conversed on the way home.

"The only other option is healing," said Pastor Jim.

"And no one wants that more than Rosie herself."

"We both know it's not beyond God's power. We believe in prayer."

"–but it must be in His timing. We can't rush God," Mary agreed.

A few months later, Jim rushed through the door holding a poster over his head. "Mary!" he called out to her. "This may be the answer we're looking for."

She took the poster from his hand and read aloud:

J.D.'s HOUR OF POWER! THE LAME WALK-THE BLIND SEE - WITNESS MIRACLES HAPPEN!

Mary looked at him with skepticism. "A healer, Jim? What about not forcing God's hand?"

"This preacher is very well known on the evangelistic circuit."

"Jim, I'm surprised at you. God doesn't need a miracle worker to perform healings."

"I know, but sometimes I think people need the extra faith of someone praying publicly for them. It sparks their own faith."

"But God can also heal when there's no faith–it has to be His choice."

Undeterred, he went on. "I'm going to call Faith to see if they saw this guy last year. I remember them being excited over some evangelist."

He picked up the phone and tapped in Faith Abrams's number.

"Good morning, Faith. Pastor Jim here. I need to ask you a question. Did you and Hope attend services last year when Reverend J.D. Blacart was in the Branson area?"

She thought a minute before answering. "We went down but he was called away by an emergency that night," said Faith.

"Tell me what you know about him."

"From what we'd heard, he travels all over the

place doing these healing meetings. Every one of them is said to be packed with people. We wanted to take Rosie to be prayed for, but it wasn't meant to be."

"You'd say he's authentic then?"

"By what others say."

"Good enough for me."

Filled with excitement and anticipation, Pastor Jim soon had J.D. Blacart booked for a week-long meeting the coming summer. He promoted the event and placed posters all over the surrounding communities.

"This may be your time," he told Rosie. "Pray and hope."

"Have faith and believe..." she finished. *And trust the wait,* she reminded herself, hopeful of what the future might bring.

40 - BAD NEWS

Rosie heard Pastor Jim and Mary talking in low voices one morning as she entered the kitchen. They stopped as soon as she came through the door.

"Good morning, sunshine." Pastor Jim tried to sound cheerful, but his somber face told her something was wrong. It bothered her all day. She wanted to ask, but was afraid, worried she'd done something wrong.

After dinner, Pastor Jim beckoned her to the living room. "No television tonight, Rose. Come sit on the couch. There's something we need to talk to you about."

Rosie put a finger into her mouth and began to chew her nails. "Am I in trouble?" she asked timidly.

"No, honey. It's about Hope." Pastor Jim was not smiling.

"Hope?" A bigger worry. "Is she okay? Is she home?"

Mary's saddened face worried her even more as she sat down beside her. Mary wrapped her arms around Rosie and patted her shoulders.

"What are you saying?" she begged, pushing Mary

away.

Pastor Jim paused to choose his words with care. “Hope fought a brave fight, but— her heart attack was too severe. The doctors did everything they could.”

“What do you mean?” Rosie’s breath came in short gasps. “She’s got to be okay. Don’t say that—” She couldn’t even finish the thought.

“I’m sorry, sweetheart,” Mary reached out to her again. “Hope’s heart was just too weak. She’s up in heaven now playing music for Jesus.”

“Hope’s dead? NO! Hope can’t die. I need her!” Rosie pulled Mary’s arms away and burst into tears.

Mary reached to comfort her, but Rosie stood, backing away. “No! It can’t be true. Please, say it isn’t true.” She shuffled to her bedroom, rubbing the tears from her eyes.

Mary started to follow, but Jim grabbed her by the hand. “Let her go. Let her cry it out. Death is a tough lesson to learn.”

“My heart breaks for her,” said Mary, her own eyes brimming.

“As does mine. But everyone must grieve in their own way.”

Rosie collapsed on the bed and sobbed. “Why, God? Why would you let Hope die? She loved you and did everything right, and... and...I loved her. Why did you take her from me? Why?"

Rosie didn't come out of her room the whole evening.

"I can't bear to leave her alone any longer," Mary said. Picking up a box of tissues, she went to Rosie's room, and knocked on the door. "Rosie? May I come in?"

Hearing a muffled reply, Mary peeked in. The girl was already in her pajamas curled into a ball on her bed. Tears streaked Rosie's face. She looked up at Mary with a questioning look. "Why, Mary? Why would God let her die?"

"It was simply Hope's time to go home. We can't know when God will call us home to be with Him." Mary sat down beside her on the bed as Rosie drew up her knees and put her chin on them. "Hope was ready to meet Jesus."

"Hope told me God doesn't let us in on His plans 'cuz He wants us to trust Him." She dabbed her face with the tissue Mary gave her.

"That's why it's good to have your heart ready all the time." She guided Rosie under the covers and tucked her in. "How about if I pray with you before you go to sleep? The Lord can give you the peace and comfort you need right now."

When Mary finished praying, she rose to leave the room.

"Mary?"

"Yes?"

"Do you think Hope can see me from heaven?"

"Why, I don't really know, honey. But she left a very special place in your heart. I imagine you still hear her words in your head from time to time. Right?" Mary gave the girl a smile and a kiss on the cheek.

"Yeah, I think of things she's said lots of times, but I'm still sad."

"Me too, honey. Me, too."

Saturday morning, Rosie's steps came slower as she entered the kitchen for breakfast. She slumped onto her chair with a frown on her face. There was no smile nor greeting. Mary set a bowl of cereal before her and sat down with her coffee.

Pastor Jim put down his newspaper when he saw the girl's downcast countenance. "What are you thinking, Rosie?" asked Pastor Jim.

"I'm mad at God." She scowled at the table, her voice croaky from crying.

"Because of Hope?"

"Mmmm-hmm."

"It was Hope's time to go home," repeated Mary.

"I don't care. I wasn't ready for her to leave." Rosie pouted.

Mary began to say something else when Jim

signaled her a 'not now' with his eyes. Rosie crossed her arms and scowled at the table, refusing to take a bite.

"You need to eat, dear."

"Not hungry."

"All right. Then put your bowl by the sink."

"No." She squinted through slits and raised her voice. "I don't have to." Rosie shoved her chair from the table, got up and stomped out of the room.

Mary gave Jim a pleading look and began to go after the girl.

"Let her go, Mary. She's working through this."

When they heard the door slam, they blinked. "She left?" Mary asked with a tilt of her head. "Should we go after her?"

"She can't go far. Let her be."

After an hour or so, Mary began to worry. Rosie had not come back into the house. She looked around in the yard. No Rosie. There was only one other probable place she could be.

Opening the rear church door, Mary heard Rosie playing, and then banging the piano keys. Playing. Pounding. Playing. Banging. Back and forth. Mary quietly walked up the steps to the main floor and stood off to the side, watching the girl take out her frustration on the piano. A melody would begin, and then Rosie banged the keys when it didn't come out right. Over and over.

"I quit. I quit. I quit!" Finally spent of energy, Rosie laid her head in her hands on the ivory keys and sobbed her heart out. Mary walked up behind her and laid her hands on the girl's shoulders.

"Cry it out, Rosie. It will cleanse your soul."

Rosie turned to face Mary with her tear-streaked face. "I'll never be able to play again."

"Rosie! Why do you say that?"

"I can't play anymore. Hope is gone – and all the music with her."

"That isn't true, dear. The music comes from within, and from above. It's a part of you."

"But Mary, you don't understand. It's all my fault."

"What is?"

"Hope died because of ME."

"How do you mean?" Mary sat down beside her on the bench and put her arm around her.

"I was too slow, Mary. My leg—" she sobbed.

"What do mean? Too slow? Rosie, you're not making sense."

"My stupid leg—it couldn't go fast enough."

"When Hope had her heart attack?"

"Yeah," Rosie wailed. "I tried to get Hope help. But...I made her *die*!"

Mary took the girl in her arms. "Oh, Rosie. You didn't make her die. It's not your fault. Hope is happy in heaven now," she soothed. "Remember what we talked about last night?"

Rosie nodded her head. "But it's so hard to trust and believe..."

"I know. Sometimes it is. That's when we have to have faith that God knows best–all the time."

"That's what Hope told me too." She sighed.

"Jim and I know how you miss Hope and your lessons," said Mary.

Rosie lifted her eyebrows and nodded. "I miss Hope more."

"Your lessons were more than just teaching music, weren't they?"

"My piano lesson was the best day of the week," said Rosie. "I waited all week just to talk to Hope. And learn to play," she added as an afterthought.

"I can give you lessons."

"But where? You don't even have a piano."

Mary smiled. "But here you are, and there's a piano. You can come to the church anytime you wish."

Mary gave her a squeeze. "Hope's funeral is tomorrow. We weren't going to make you go with us, but you're welcome to come if you want."

"I want to," said Rosie.

That night Rosie prayed an earnest, heartfelt prayer. Relaxing under the warm, fuzzy blankets, she thanked the Lord for her foster parents and the home she shared with them. And although still sad about Hope, she felt she had her very own angel to smile down upon her and give her a special hope.

"God, I want to come to heaven someday and see You—and Hope too. Come into my heart and make me ready to meet you."

41 – CURSED

The next morning, Rosie felt as if she was wrapped up safe in God's embrace. For the first time in her twelve years, she felt at peace. Sitting up in bed, she stretched her arms out wide and looked upward. "I love you, God. Thank you for your peace and your love. She wrapped her arms around herself and squeezed. "Thank you for becoming my Father! I've always wanted a father to love me. And God," she said as she eased out of bed, "if You can do anything about this stupid leg, that really would be a miracle!"

Mary found Jim in his basement study room the morning of the funeral, putting the final edits on Hope's memorial. She told him about her conversation with Rosie the night before.

"She's coming around," said Mary. "It's hard to believe she thought she caused Hope's death."

At that moment, they were startled by a chilling scream coming from the bathroom. Both Jim and Mary ran up the basement stairs two at a time, hearts in their throats.

"NO! No. No. No. NO! NO! God please!" Rosie's cried out.

"Rosie! What's wrong?" Mary found the girl in the bathroom doubled over, clutching her stomach with blood running down her legs. A small puddle of blood lay beneath her. "ROSIE! What did you do to yourself?"

"I'm DYING, Mary! Just like Nina told me! I'm cursed!"

Mary cocked her head and frowned, but she gathered her composure as she quickly looked the girl over. Finding no injuries, she enfolded Rosie in her arms. Giving Jim a knowing look, she patted him on the arm and backed him out the door. "I've got this one, dear." She turned back to Rosie who was still wild-eyed and in pain. "My dear girl, you're not cursed."

"Nina said I was." Her breaths came in panicked gasps. "Cursed by the devil when he kissed me."

Mary's eyes widened in shock "She really said that?"

Rosie nodded. "Then why am I bleeding to death?"

"I seriously didn't think we'd have to have this talk so soon after you got here," she said mostly to herself. "You are becoming a woman, Rosie. That's all it is. You won't bleed to death. Take your shower, and I'll explain it all when you're done."

Mary was ready with hygiene products when Rosie came out of the shower. After she was dressed, they sat on the edge of her bed and had a woman-to-woman talk.

"I thought God was mad at me. Or that the devil kicked me again."

"Rosie, where do you get such thoughts?" Mary shook her head.

"That's what Nina always told me," she said as a matter-of-fact. "The devil kicked me to make me so lame I couldn't run away. Then he gave me the devil's kiss to make me his own."

"Wha-a-at? The what? What did you call it?" Mary was aghast.

"The devil's kiss. Nina said it was his mark of evil." She ran her finger over the scar.

"Oh, my sweet Rose." Mary cupped the girl's face. "It's only a bad scar."

Rosie shook her head. "Nina said it no man would ever want someone with the devil's kiss. It makes me ugly. Besides, no one ever loves a cripple."

Mary shook her head. "We love you Rosie. Unconditionally. Always and forever." Mary hugged Rosie, and then released her hold. "Nina never told you what really happened to your face, or why your leg is lame?"

"Nuh-uh. I wanted to believe I was born this way. It made me want to puke when I thought the devil might have kissed me."

Mary put her hand to her breast and made a quick decision. "Rosie, I think you're old enough to know what really happened."

Mary shared the story of how Rosie and her mother were in a car accident, and then how her mother died. "So, you see, dear child, you're a survivor. Don't you ever forget it. The mark on your face is your badge of courage; it's your mark of beauty. It shows your determination to live and that you were strong enough to defy death."

"So — the devil never gave me this scar?"

"Never."

That afternoon, Rosie felt a little scared to see Hope so still in the casket. It was almost more than she could bear. Touching the older woman's cold, folded hands made her jump. But then, she noticed the calm look on the woman's face with close to a smile on her lips. She stood at the casket a long time gazing upon the face of her older friend.

"She looks so peaceful... almost as if she's asleep, doesn't she?" asked Faith who nuzzled in beside her.

"She does. And she looks happy, too. But I miss her so much."

"So do I, sweetie." Tears ran down her cheeks as Faith squeezed Rosie. She was my only sibling."

Rosie tucked more tissues into Faith's hand and

hugged her long and hard. “Faith, I want to thank you. You and Hope were the first ones who taught me about faith. You gave me hope when I didn’t have any and helped me learn how to trust the wait. And because of both of you, I’m going to heaven too, someday.

As Pastor Jim came up from behind, Rosie released her hold on Faith, and blinked away her own tears. She looked up at him with a feeble smile.

“You doing okay, honey?” he asked.

“I am now,” she said.

42 - THE MAN WITH THE GOLDEN HANDS

Rosie learned her piano skills well over the winter months as she practiced daily. Along with her natural talent and God-given gift, she blossomed as a pianist.

When Mary told Rosie they wanted her to be the pianist for the tent meetings, she didn't know whether to be happy, scared, or thankful. She had never played before a large crowd before, only the small evening services at church. During the week, she went after school every day to practice the hymns and choruses. She loved the way the piano strings echoed in the empty sanctuary.

Many times, Pastor Jim found her creating a beautiful song of praise. "Rosie is a natural, Mary. A real prodigy. Her music touches me deep in my soul."

"That I know. She has a real gift," said Mary, "and she's developed far beyond what I could ever play. She'll do fine for the tent meetings."

The day J.D. Blacart's motorhome and semi rolled into town, Pastor Jim had high anticipations. Property had been reserved outside of town for the big tent with plenty of room for parking.

"We're excited to have you in our area, Reverend

Blacart. You have quite a reputation," said Pastor Jim. "I'll be on hand for anything you need. My name is Pastor Jim." He held out his hand.

Blacart disregarded the pastor's hand and lifted his head. "Well, Jim, as one preacher to another, we'll make it a good show." The man in the black Stetson shouted to the men setting up the tent posts. "Get that one straighter," he pointed out, walking past the pastor.

Pastor Jim cocked his head at the statement and followed behind. "I'm curious. Why the tent? Isn't a tent outdated?"

The preacher rubbed his hands on his blue jeans and raised his sunglasses to look Pastor Jim in the eye. "Oh, sure it is. That's the point. It's a huge visual draw to the community." He raised his arms skyward. "It's a reminder to people that this is the tent of meeting–a place to meet with God." The man lowered his voice. "It's also a crowd-getter because people are curious to come and see what happens."

Pastor Jim tipped his head. "Sounds like you've been asked that question before. You rattled off that answer in a fast clip."

Blacart hooted. "You could say that."

"Shepherd's Creek church will provide the music. My daughter will be playing the piano. Wait until you hear her. She is a phenomenon," Pastor Jim said as he followed Blacart around the tent.

"Um-hmm," Blacart responded with distraction as he inspected the workers and gave orders to the laborious chair and platform setup.

"What brought you down this path, Reverend? I mean, traveling around the country doing tent meetings? Wouldn't it be a more stable life to settle down somewhere and minister in a church?"

Blacart's disturbing laugh turned to scorn as he gave his reply. "As a kid, I attended an old-fashioned tent meeting out of curiosity. The speaker was dynamic and a powerfully skilled orator. It intrigued and mystified me when he touched people and they fell over." In demonstrative motions, he portrayed each statement. "Blind people regained their sight, and the lame walked. People jumped out of wheelchairs and ran down the aisles. It was a grand slam." He spread his arms wide. "I wanted to try my luck and see if I could do it too. People enjoy a good show and what better place than under a tent in the open air?" He pointed to the tent being raised. "Let me be the first to say I'm good at what I do. I won't disappoint."

"So...." Pastor Jim adjusted his glasses as if to focus on the troublesome testimony. "Would you say God called you into this ministry?"

The question seemed to puzzle Blacart as he stumbled a second for words. "Well, my dear man, aren't we all 'called'?" He slapped Pastor Jim on the back. "Now, if you'll excuse me, I need to prepare for tonight's service."

He left Pastor Jim standing in the dirt with a punch-in-the-gut uneasy feeling.

As Rosie prepared herself for the first night's services, her hand shook as she tried to brush her hair.

"You can do this, sweetie," encouraged Mary. "I've watched you play. When you start to worship, it's almost as if you're not the one who's playing." Mary took the brush and ran it through Rosie's black curls.

Rosie giggled nervously. "That's how I feel too!"

"You'll be great. Just let the Lord play through your fingers."

As Mary brushed Rosie's hair behind her ear, the bristles touched the scar making it puffy and red. Rosie reached up and pushed her finger against it. "I hate this ugly scar."

"I think we can cover it up," Mary dabbed a touch of concealer on the scar. "There. Now you can hardly see it. Look."

Rosie viewed her image in the mirror. Mary had covered the scar well.

"Remember what I told you. That scar is your message of beauty. Let it define you, Rosie. Wear it proudly. You're a survivor."

Rosie tossed her black curls behind her ears and over her shoulder. Standing tall, she smiled at a whole new image in the mirror. *My beauty mark.*

On the opening night of the crusade, the amazing J.D. Blacart ran from the back of the tent with a whoop and a holler. The spotlight sparkled off his white rhinestone-studded jacket. "Tonight is YOUR night!" he shouted. The microphone screeched. "Are you ready?" Louder, he yelled, "I said, are you R-E-A-D-Y?"

The people jumped to their feet clapping and hollering. He dazzled the crowds with his staged miracles and smoothly-oiled tongue. The "Man with the Golden Hands" had taken Ridgetown by storm.

Playing before a big crowd made Rosie nervous at first, but she soon found that her fingers glided across the ivories with hardly any effort. She felt as if Hope was smiling down on her, and she knew God was. She closed her eyes and became engrossed in the music. It felt as if her fingers became an extension of God's Hands. All she had to do was worship and let her fingers find the keys.

"Have you heard the girl play?" J.D. Blacart overheard one person ask another on their way into the tent.

“She is amazing,” replied the other.

“Music straight from heaven.”

“If she doesn’t know the song, the song leader only has to sing it once, and she picks it up and begins to play.”

Blacart agreed. Rosie was a wonderful pianist. People were coming more to hear this girl play than to see his performance of staged miracles. For some reason, this crippled girl touched a deeply hidden soft spot in his heart from the first night he saw her hobble onto the platform. He wished the power of healing really was in his hands as everyone said.

After a couple of nights of services, Pastor Jim expressed concern with his wife. “Something seems out of place here, but I can’t put my finger on it.”

“You mean about Reverend Blacart? The services seem to be going very well. People enjoy Rosie’s music and the reverend’s preaching. He is very charismatic. People are being blessed and healed.”

“That’s how it appears but something in my gut feels wrong.”

43 - THE GIFT

Although the crusade meetings were in full swing every night, it didn't stop the normal everyday events. "Ms. Anders is here for you, Rose," called Mary. "She says she has something special planned today."

"Okay," she shrugged as she got into the car with the caseworker. It wasn't unusual for her caseworker to check in on her from time to time. She wasn't worried, but it did make her wonder. She hoped she wouldn't have to leave the Davises, but Ms. Anders once told her this was only a temporary placement.

From Davis's home in Ridgetown, Ms. Anders steered the car north toward Queen City. Rosie was curious when they pulled into the parking lot of Resthaven Senior Residential Care. They entered the front door and stopped at the desk.

"Raymond Gavotte, please?"

"He's always in the community room this time of day–down the hall to the right. Is he expecting you?"

"Yes, he is. We're here for a short visit."

"Rose," said Ms. Anders. "This man you're about to meet will be a very important part of your life."

Her heart skipped a beat. Immediately her mind

shot back to the time when Nina wanted to introduce her to 'a very important man.' Rosie slowed her pace behind the caseworker.

Ms. Anders didn't seem to notice and chattered on. "Mr. Gavotte was once the Mayor of Queen City. He wants to meet you." Ms. Anders took the girl aside before entering the community room. They sat together on a side bench.

"Mayor? Why me?" her tiny voice squeaked, the old familiar fear creeping in again.

"Because—" she paused long and searched Rosie's eyes, "he has something to give you." Ms. Anders touched the girl's hand. "There is nothing to worry about, Rose. I'll be right there by you."

Rosie took a deep breath and then bit her lip. She calmed down some but was still filled with apprehension. She closed her eyes and said a quick silent prayer. She heard Hope's voice in her head again: *Be brave, hold on to faith....* She took a huge breath and with new courage, lifted herself from the bench. "Okay. I'm ready."

As they entered the room, they passed a baby grand piano in the corner. She slid her fingers across the slick ebony finish and then touched a couple of ivory keys. Several older men played cards at one table, another woman worked on a jigsaw puzzle, and many watched "Jeopardy" on television. An older man with silvery hair sat in a wheelchair facing the bay window, enjoying the birds fluttering on the birdbath outside. The sunlight caught the silver in his hair, making it glimmer.

"There he is, Rose," whispered Ms. Anders, pointing to the man by the window. "Let's go meet him."

He's in a wheelchair? He can't walk right either? Somehow the wheelchair made all the difference in the world. Her anxieties left as she relaxed. Ms. Anders walked over and touched his shoulder.

"Mr. Gavotte? We're here."

Raymond Gavotte wheeled around to greet them. He looked up at Ms. Anders. As he gazed upon the girl standing before him, laugh crinkles appeared around his eyes as his lips curved into a deeply satisfied smile. "Well, hello there."

The deepness of his voice made her feel warm and safe. Rosie blushed and looked at the floor, self-consciously pulling her hair over her left cheek.

"This is Rose Delahunt, Carmen's daughter," said Ms. Anders.

"Rose. A beautiful name for a beautiful girl," he said, nodding with approval. "Let me look at you, Rose." He reached for her hand.

Timidly, she offered her hand and then gazed into the kindest sky-blue eyes she had ever seen.

"I'm so sorry we haven't met before."

What's he talking about? She shyly eased her hand away put it over her scar. *I don't understand.*

"Sit and tell me about yourself." He patted the folding chair Ms. Anders had put by him.

Suddenly tongue-tied, she gave Ms. Anders a bewildered look and shrugged.

"Tell him about your piano playing, Rose," encouraged Ms. Anders.

With a look of relief, she said quietly, "I just learned to play the piano. It's something I can do without my leg getting in the way."

"Ms. Anders tells me you are an excellent pianist."

Rosie beamed. "I love to play. It feels like my fingers make music by themselves. It's hard to explain. I just feel it."

"I would love to hear you. Would you tickle the ivories for me?"

"Here?" she sat back in surprise.

"Do you need music? There's music inside the piano bench," said Mr. Gavotte.

"No," she giggled. "I play by ear most of the time. If you want to know the truth, I wanted to play that piano the moment I saw it. What would you like to hear?"

"Anything you wish, my dear."

"A hymn then? I play those best."

Rosie hobbled over to the piano, sat down, and began to play. Closing her eyes, she became absorbed in the tunes emanating from her fingers. Her rendition of "Amazing Grace" soon captured the entire room.

"I'm glad you changed your mind about meeting your granddaughter, Mr. Gavotte," said Ms. Anders while they listened to Rosie play.

"I almost made another rash decision I'd forever regret," he admitted. "Once I thought it over, there wasn't any reason not to meet my only grandchild. I'd be foolish not to take this opportunity."

"She's an amazing girl," said Ms. Anders.

"What's wrong with her leg?"

"A car accident when she was a toddler; the same one that put your daughter in a coma."

"So sad. I know her pain," he said. "Nothing like being a cripple with a brilliant mind."

Mr. Gavotte leaned back and enjoyed her music for a few moments. Rosie looked toward him while she played and smiled. He nodded his approval and returned the smile.

"Her music draws her out, does it not? She is phenomenal, like you said, Ms. Anders."

When Rosie finished her song, everyone in the room applauded. It brought a smile of satisfaction to her face. She painfully lifted herself from the bench and hobbled back by Mr. Gavotte.

"Your playing is incredible—a genuine gift." His old eyes twinkled.

"Thank you." She ducked her head and blushed.

"I'm glad you came today. Mr. Gavotte searched her face and Rosie felt a shiver go through her. He took both of Rosie's hands in his and lifted his face upward. "Bless these hands, Lord. Thank You, for the gift You've given to her."

His large hands felt like soft leather enfolding hers as he gently held them to his chest. Rosie scrunched her forehead and wondered what was happening.

Mr. Gavotte cleared his throat and seemed to have trouble forming words. He patted the chair beside him. "Will you sit down by me? I have something very important to tell you."

She flashed Ms. Anders a questioning look.

"It's okay, Rose, I'll be on the other side of the room," said Ms. Anders. Turning to the man in the wheelchair she said, "I'll go get some coffee so you and Rose may speak privately."

"What is it, Mr. Gavotte?" Rosie saw tears starting to form in his eyes. "Are you okay?" Anxious thoughts turned to her last day with Hope as she sat down beside him.

He dug his handkerchief from his pocket to dab at his old eyes. Clearing his throat, he began to speak, but then seemed at a loss for words. Now he was the one who was tongue-tied. "You and I...." he choked, "...we are...uh...You are...."

"What is it, Mr. Gavotte? Are you sick?" Rosie's worries grew thinking of Hope slumping over the keyboard.

He cleared his throat again. "My dear child," he looked in her eyes, "I'm not sure... how to tell you this."

Rosie wrinkled her forehead, feeling strangely drawn to him as he searched her face. His eyes were kind and loving, not like Benny's longing look, or the old man's evil eye. On impulse, she reached over and touched his hand. "It's okay, Mr. Gavotte."

The older man studied her innocent eyes. "I... am..." The words caught in his throat, "... your... grandfather."

Rosie's eyes widened. She stood to her feet as her mouth dropped open. Her hands flew to her chest. "How? How can that be?"

"Your mother, Carmen... she was my daughter."

"Nina never said anything about you. W-w-hy are you telling me this now?" Rosie grew quiet as she sat again and took in his features in a brand-new way. The light from the window made his silver hair shine; his upper lip was almost covered by his mustache.

He sighed deeply and the tension in the room eased. "Your grandmother left me when Carmen was a little girl. Part of that is my fault..." He let out a long breath. "...and my regret. I didn't find out about you until two months ago." He patted her hands. "I so wish things could've been different."

A real grandfather? Rosie tried to wrap her mind around the news. Her heart leapt with new hope of family.

"Perhaps if I would have known about you when you were younger, your life would have turned out better."

Suddenly aware she was staring, Rosie quickly turned her gaze to the floor. "I don't remember my mother." Her voice reflected sadness. "And Nina...." She couldn't finish the sentence as old memories crept back.

"I don't remember much of your mother either. She was young when your grandmother left. But one thing I do see in you..."

"What?" Rosie leaned in with new anticipation. The quiet richness of his voice made her feel like she was wrapped in warm fuzzies.

"You have your mother's smile and her cute little nose. You're such a beauty, my dear." He touched his finger to her nose making it crinkle.

Rosie blushed and giggled, making him laugh out loud.

"Will you come back and play for me again sometime?"

His melodious deep laugh filled her with joy. Her eyes brightened as she broke into a grin. "I will if I can–especially now that I know my *grandfather* lives here!"

"Good. Good. Now before you go, I have a special gift for you."

"Nothing could be more special than God giving me the gift of a real grandfather!" Rosie bubbled.

Raymond Gavotte smiled with pleasure and pulled a check from his shirt pocket. Handing it to her, he said, "Follow your dreams, my sweet flower."

She looked to Ms. Anders for approval and then took the check from his hand. As she read it, she began to laugh and cry at the same time. "Tuition for Sunshine Music Academy? Really?"

"A full four-year scholarship after you finish high school, my dear. Learn to sing, dance, or learn to play an instrument, if you want. You will live there, you'll learn, and your future will be secure," Mr. Gavotte beamed.

"Oh, Grandfather!" Rosie leaned down and put her arms around his neck. "Thank you, thank you, thank you."

"All for you. Live your dreams, child. It's the least I can do."

As they left the residential home, Rosie couldn't stop jabbering about her newfound grandfather, the scholarship, and the academy. Everything bubbled up inside and spilled out with joy. Then she thought of Nina.

"What will Nina say? Are you going to tell her about the scholarship?" she asked Ms. Anders. "Are you going to tell her about Grandfather Gavotte?"

"I don't need to tell her anything. And you won't have to worry about it either. You won't be seeing your grandmother for a good long while."

44 – WAITING

It was Thursday night of the week-long crusade with J.D. Blacart. It took Rusty most of the week to build up enough courage to approach Blacart. The words of her friend 'His words are as slick as oil; he can slip out of anything' gave her cold feet. Time was running out—only two more days of meetings. She wanted to expose this fraud in front of the biggest crowd possible.

She passed a man in a black suit standing at the back of the tent. Catching a glimpse of his badge, she assumed he was part of Blacart's security team. She gave him a nod, found a seat on the back row and sat to listen to the heavenly music coming from the piano. She strained to get a better look at the pianist but from the back, she couldn't make out any features.

"She plays like an angel, doesn't she?" the lady sitting next to her commented.

"Who is she?"

"The pastor's daughter—the child prodigy. Word has it she's only been playing for a few months."

Rusty closed her eyes and tried to enjoy the melodies but strategizing on how to take the preacher man down filled her mind instead.

Up front, Pastor Jim confided in his wife as people filled the tent. “I still can’t shake this feeling. Something’s off.”

“I feel it too, Jim. Blacart doesn’t appear authentic. He’s too theatrical. Too...” she tapped her finger on her mouth to produce the right word, “too...”

“... too phony.” He finished her sentence. “I’m going to confront him after service and see what he has to say for himself.”

“Do you think that’s wise? Maybe you should take someone with you.”

“Are you volunteering?” He gave his wife a squeeze and a grin.

“I’m serious. Perhaps you should have another man as a backup. Better yet, a policeman.”

“Do you think there’ll be a dispute?” He gave her a quick peck on the cheek. “On the other hand, I know you have keen discernment and you hear from the Lord. I will heed your warning as if it came from God Himself.”

Pastor Jim made his rounds greeting the people as they came in. He approached the man in a black suit standing at the back, introduced himself, and invited him to find a seat.

“Nice to meet you, Pastor Jim, but I prefer to

stand. I get a better view." The detective flashed his badge for the pastor. "I'm on duty."

"I didn't realize J.D. had a police detail here all week," said Pastor Jim.

"Oh, no. I'm not working for the reverend. I'm investigating him."

"I'm afraid to ask why." Pastor Jim clenched his teeth. "... but I think I know."

"If it was my choice, Pastor, I wouldn't have come to this type of meeting. But I was asked to investigate a few things regarding the preacher. I hope you understand."

"I do," he said as he held out his hand. "I need to confront him about a few things myself. If you could spare a few minutes after the meeting, I would like to talk to you about it."

Flanders agreed, shook the pastor's hand, and continued to watch the people enter. As a redhead passed in front of him, he followed her with his eyes, taking note of where she sat. Something about her looked vaguely familiar. He searched his brain for where he'd seen her before. *Is this the infamous Rusty Delahunt?*

He recalled Ms. Anders's conversation from earlier in the day. Rusty Delahunt had worked out a plea bargain with the court and was cooperating with them on several counts. Hearing Blacart was in the area, she had called Ms. Anders to fill her in on what she knew of the man. Ms. Anders said Rusty had damning information on Blacart that would expose him as a fraud and cheat. She wanted to help take the man down.

"How would she know he's a fraud?" Flanders remembered asking.

"Knows him from her past. Met him at Benny's Place over a decade ago." Ms. Anders had waited a minute for that to sink in.

"How did she remember him from that long ago?"

"Said her daughter met Blacart when she was a teenager–at Benny's Place."

"J.D. Blacart?"

"The same. Says he's Rosie's father."

"J.D. is Rosie's father?" he repeated. "You're not serious!"

"Dead serious. Rusty's determined to prove it and then expose him as a charlatan before the whole crowd. Says he's deceiving people with his lies and then swindling them out of their money. Says she's going to the meeting ready to take him down. I need you to be there in case there's any action."

45 – SUSPICIONS

Flanders sat eagle-eyed, scrutinizing every move, looking for any clue of evidence as he watched J.D. Blacart expound upon the Word. The preaching was boisterous, J.D.'s actions flashy as he stomped, spit, and shouted from one side of the platform to the other. Flanders was there to witness the man's methods, to take notes but nothing more. He was amused yet mystified. When the helpers ushered in a friend of his parents in a wheelchair, his eyebrows raised. The frail, seventy-ish Mrs. Murphy kept her body slightly bent forward with her shoulders slumped. She held her head in her hands as if in pain. *That's strange. When I saw her last week, Mrs. Murphy wasn't crippled, paralyzed, or hurt.*

Blacart knew how to preach and how to persuade the crowd, as evidenced when the offering baskets were passed. People emptied their pockets and purses. Flanders grimaced with a clenched jaw, confounded as Blacart pled for more and more money. When one offering didn't yield the desired amount, he demanded another.

"Fifty dollars buys a blessing; one hundred dollars guarantees healing! Don't be stingy. Give. Let God multiply your blessings!" Blacart yelled into the microphone. "Give and it shall be given to you! Shaken down. Pressed together and RUNNING over!"

Something didn't mesh here. Flanders leaned forward watching the preacher called one person after another to the front for healing. Blacart lifted his head toward the sky and tightly closed his eyes as if reading peoples' minds.

Then J.D. pointed to Mrs. Murphy, sitting limply in her wheelchair. "Bring that woman in the front row to the platform," he directed the ushers.

An excited little 'ooooh' escaped Mrs. Murphy's lips. She clapped her hands to her mouth as they began to wheel her forward.

"Your legs have weakened from years in this chair, isn't that right?" J.D. asked her.

She nodded with big puppy-dog eyes.

"And you've been told you'll never walk again. True?"

She forced tears to her eyes. She nodded again, dabbing her face with a tissue.

"I tell you, madam, tonight is YOUR night. You *will* walk again." He reached for her hands. "Come."

He lifted her by the hand in slow dramatic motion. "Walk, madam." He pulled her forward, making her step away from the wheelchair. "WALK!" He led her back and forth across the platform.

The crowd oohed and ahhed. J.D. was on a roll. "Who's next? You, there in the purple shirt," he pointed. "Step UP and RECEIVE your HEALING."

Without a hitch, Blacart kept up the facade, creating wild pandemonium amongst the astounded crowd. Shouts! Cheers! Applause!

Flanders felt gall in his throat. He glanced at the redhead. She had the same reaction. A flash of recognition registered in his head. To make sure, he pulled his cellphone from his pocket and flipped through his photos until he found those from the wall in Benny's Place. An older model of the same woman sat on the back row. He scrolled back through his pictures taken at Rusty's house. He found the younger version. Before him sat Rusty Delahunt in the flesh. The service was almost over. He had to make his move now.

"This seat open?" he asked as he slipped in beside her on the back row.

She nodded.

"Excuse me for being so forward, ma'am. Are you Rusty Delahunt?"

Rusty whirled about with alarm, blooding draining from her face. "Ye..aahh?" she answered slowly, ready to bolt.266

"I'm Detective John Flanders." He flashed his badge. "Heard you were here to expose the preacher."

46 – INVESTIGATION

Rusty felt so lightheaded she thought she would faint. She tried to shake her head to deny the allegation, but it wouldn't move. "W-w-who–who told you that?" she stuttered.

"Let's just say we have a mutual acquaintance, Stacey Anders from CPS?"

"She sent you after me?" She jumped up to leave. "Thought we had a deal."

Flanders put his hand on her shoulder and lowered her back onto the chair. "Don't worry. I'm not here for you. Stay after the service so we can talk. Don't do anything tonight, okay?"

Shaking, Rusty nodded in confusion.

Flanders settled into his chair beside her, making sure she wouldn't leave. When the final amen was given, he turned toward the woman. "Listen, Ms. Delahunt. I'm not here to arrest you. I don't even intend to stop you from whatever you're planning. We're here for the same reason–to take this fraud down, but we need a plan."

Rusty relaxed her tensed shoulders. She tilted her head as she pushed her red curls behind her ear. "I already have a plan."

"We need real proof on Blacart. But right now,

I must find a couple of people before they leave. Stay put until I come back? Don't leave, please," he warned.

"I'll wait," she said more out of curiosity than consideration.

Flanders searched for Mrs. Murphy and found her in a line with several others moving toward a small area behind the platform. He hurried to catch up to her.

"Mrs. Murphy," he called to her.

She turned toward the man's voice. "Johnny Flanders! Well, look at you, all grown up. It's been ages."

"Yes, it has."

"How are your folks?"

"They're fine. Still living north of Queen City in Springdale. You're quite a ways from home, aren't you?"

"Just came down for the meeting."

"Listen. I need to ask you something that's been bothering me tonight. I didn't know you were having problems with your legs. Didn't I see you at the Queen City farmer's market last week? You were walking fine there."

"Oh," she tittered, "that's right. I did see you last

week, didn't I? Oh, my legs are just fine."

"The reverend implied your legs were weakened from years in the wheelchair. You agreed and stated you were afraid you'd never walk again."

"A slight exaggeration," she snickered. "You know, for the show."

"The show?"

"It's *all* just a show, John." Her voice dripped with sarcasm.

Flanders cocked his head sideways but feigned interest. While walking to a covered area behind the platform, they engaged in chitchat. Flanders saw many people who were supposedly healed during the services. Each one was receiving a check.

"Mrs. Murphy, what's all this?"

"Oh, Reverend Blacart pays all the actors," she said, "and I need the extra money."

Flanders discreetly snapped some pictures with his phone and then flipped on the recorder.

"You mean all the people who appeared to be healed here tonight are paid actors?"

"Oh, John. You're *so* serious," Mrs. Murphy pooh-poohed. "Of course, they're actors. Reverend Blacart wouldn't be so foolish to bring someone up front who actually needed to be healed."

"I see." Flanders cleared his throat, fighting to keep control of his astonishment. "And he pays these people?" He made sure to record every word.

"Yes. Are you interested? He needs new people every night. Tomorrow night will be the biggest and best, and he needs lots of performers."

"Hmm. A very good plan, Mrs. Murphy. Thank you for the idea."

"Go see the man over there," she pointed. "He will sign you up, prep you, and tell you what you have to do. Good seeing you, John. Tell your mom and dad hello for me."

What luck. This will make things a lot easier. He signed up for the Friday night meeting and added Rusty's name to the list. Their assignment was to play the role of a couple; she would be blind with a white red-tipped cane; he would be her guide and helper. This would get them up front together. Flanders was eager to formulate their strategy to take down the phony preacher man.

But first, he had an appointment with Pastor Jim.

47 – CONFRONTATION

"Reverend Blacart," Pastor Jim caught up with him hurrying to his motor home after the service. "I need to speak to you."

Blacart kept walking, ignoring the pastor.

Pastor Jim broke into stride with the preacher. "Now I realize why you like a tent for your show."

J.D. stopped and turned toward him with an irritated look.

"It's a complete three-ring circus."

"You said it right the first time." J.D. flicked a piece of lint from his sparkly white coat. "It's a show. Never said it was anything less. People like shows. They want entertainment at any cost. They love the fantastic and want to believe. So, I give them what they want–the fantastic. I tell them what they like to hear, and they believe anything. And they even pay me for it!" He threw back his head in a howl.

The preacher's irreverent laugh sent a shiver up Pastor Jim's back. His mouth dropped open. "You admit it?"

"Sure. I admit it. Tell me you don't do the same thing," J.D. curled his lip in a sneer. "This stuff isn't real. We have to put it on."

Pastor Jim flinched as the creepy-crawly settled on his neck and stood his hairs on end. He sent up a silent prayer for help and then stepped in front of Blacart with the boldness of God. He put his finger in Blacart's face, stopping him short. "You're wrong, Blacart. God is real. His power is true. A wise person will not mock Him or His power. Real miracles exist for believers. Your pretense brings you honor from people, but it is an abomination in the sight of God."

"You know, Jim," J.D.'s tone was condescending although his face showed a pretense of sincerity, "I really wish I *could* feel the power of God like people say. If I could touch your daughter and see her leg straighten, then maybe I *would* believe in miracles."

Pastor Jim felt his face turn red as hot anger rose within. His hands clenched. "It's not *your* hands that heal, mister." Quivering on the inside, he glared at the preacher without blinking. Taking a deep breath, he challenged, "If God could use a donkey to deliver His message, then He can use anything–even a phony like you. You are very small if you think miracles come from your 'golden hands'. Real healing comes from God. You wear a noble, pious expression in public, but God knows your heart, and it matches your name."

The men now stood face to face–eye to eye. J.D. sneered as he looked down his nose at Pastor Jim. "I've never claimed to be a preacher–or a man of God. Other people call me that. I've never claimed to have golden hands or to heal anyone. People believe what they see–real or not. I can't help it if they want to throw their money at me." He opened the door of his motor home. "Good night, Jim."

"Someday, you will see and feel the real Presence of God, mister. On that day, you'd better bow your knee and repent of your sins."

"We'll see about that," said J.D. as he went inside his motor home and slammed the door.

"Yep. We'll see about that," said Pastor Jim to himself.

"Did you get all that?" Pastor Jim asked the detective, who was hiding nearby in the shadows.

"Yep. Got it all on my recorder. Good job."

"Thanks for agreeing to back me up."

"No, thank *you*," said Flanders. "Your conversation here sealed the deal. I have all the evidence I need."

Flanders found Rusty waiting in nervous anxiety for him outside the tent. People mingled, chatted, and bought JDB trinkets as she paced back and forth.

"It makes me want to vomit," Rusty spat.

"I know what you mean. It's not right, or legal.

He's a swindler and a fraud, and now I have his own words to prove it." He patted his cellphone.

"I can prove it too," said Rusty. "That wretched man impregnated my daughter and then, as far as I'm concerned, caused her death."

"How can you prove it? Your daughter is dead." Flanders was blunt.

"Carmen's daughter is proof enough."

"Does he know about her?"

Rusty told him about the letter she had written to Blacart the previous year. "I warned him then I would expose him if I got the chance. But he ditched town before I could pull it off."

"Do you still have the letter?"

"I have a copy." She pointed to her purse. "I gave him the original. I wish Rosie could be here so I could point her out to him."

"Let's hope we don't have to drag her into this mess. At any rate, we have our roles to play tomorrow night. This will get us up to the platform in front of him. From there, we'll improvise. Let's get some coffee and talk this through."

Rusty's head exploded. *It's finally going to happen.*

"Mary," Pastor Jim called to her when he came home.

"You won't believe this guy. He actually admitted he's a phony." He threw his keys onto the table and sank down onto a kitchen chair.

"And you're still going through with the final meeting?" she asked.

"We have to. We've billed it as the largest-attended meeting of the week. People are coming from everywhere. It also means it will be the most widely witnessed takedown ever. People must know they've been deceived. We must stop this devil from doing it again."

Mary brought him a cup of coffee and sat down across from him. "But somehow," she cautioned, "you must also assure the people that the power of God is still true and worth believing."

Pastor Jim wagged his head. "Mary, how could I have been such a dunce? So blindsided? The first day J.D. came, he practically told me he wasn't the real deal. His words to me: 'I'm good at what I do. I'll put on a grand show and draw in the crowds.' Why couldn't I see it then?"

"Even the devil knows the Word of God and has a lot of tricks in his bag. He's an enemy who comes to steal, kill, and destroy. We must be wise and alert people to the enemy's deceptions, even when the enemy is a wolf in sheep's clothing."

"Well, no more cons for this guy. We'll strip him so

bare no one will ever give money to him again." Pastor Jim pursed his lips, adamant to follow through.

48 – CORNERED

It was the last night of the week-long meetings. Rosie was sad to see it end. It filled her with such pleasure to play the piano and see how her music blessed the people. She felt God's pleasure, too, and knew Hope must be smiling at her.

She was curious why the preacher had not called her to the front for healing like he had the others. She wanted to go forward every night but was too timid. Pride, embarrassment, and shame held her back. Now she kicked herself for not having taken the first step. Pastor Jim and Mary reminded her it was all in God's time. She had to trust the wait. *Maybe tonight....* She hoped.

She put on the red dress Hope and Faith had bought her and on impulse, grabbed the gold scarf. She pulled her black curls loosely back and tied them with a silk bow, no longer ashamed of the scar. Mary's encouraging words were replacing Nina's cruel ones. *Not the devil's kiss. It's my mark of beauty. A sign that God spared my life for something special.*

"Here's tonight's list, Brother Blacart," said one of the

workers. "Anything else you need?"

He looked over the list: descriptions of the actors, their maladies to be healed, and their seating assignments. "No. Think we're good here."

J.D. watched the crowd file in by the tens and then by the hundreds. More wheelchairs lined the aisles after so many people saw Mrs. Murphy rise from her wheeled prison and walk across the platform the night before. Surveying the audience, Blacart located each of the recruited performers on the list.

A redhead entered tapping her white cane back and forth on the ground with a man who supported her by the arm. J.D. took note of her seat: fifth row, middle aisle. This 'blind woman' would regain her eyesight tonight.

J.D. watched the pastor's daughter hobble onto the platform. She settled onto the piano bench and smiled sweetly at him. It flustered him for some reason. He observed the girl as she played. Jonathan Blacart felt a strange new compassion but shook himself as other thoughts entered his evil mind. *She sets the mood. Brings them in. Like magic. They come to see her, not me. Hmmm. I could use her.* Feeling a new electrified energy in the crowd, he shivered but didn't know why.

Pastor Jim took his place on the platform beside Blacart. The tension was thick between them.

Rosie's spirit had been restless all week. Even though it seemed miracles were evident night after night, tonight seemed different. She felt the Holy Spirit in an atmosphere of hope and expectancy. As she began to play, a holy and awesome power seemed to blossom from her innermost being. She lifted her head heavenward and closed her eyes. Her fingers danced across the keys, without her being aware of where they moved, transporting her to heavenly places. Soon her angelic music filled the tent.

"You ready?" Flanders whispered.

"Yes, I have my prop." While staring straight ahead she tapped the red-tipped white cane she'd brought with her. "All set." She went over the plan in her head one more time.

Flanders surveyed the tent for his plain-clothed officers. They were stationed around the perimeter, awaiting his cue to move in.

Vigorous jumping, dancing, and loud singing exploded through the night air as people seemed wired for action. Rosie felt the power and electricity in the air. Her spirit elevated with anticipation. When the song service was finished, Rosie rose to her feet and began to move toward her seat in the front row.

Pastor Jim stepped up to the pulpit. "Thank you,

Rose. We have been blessed by your wonderful playing this week. Your gift from God is truly felt by all of us here."

The crowd applauded, and the girl blushed with pleasure. She looked over at her foster father and gave him a cute shrug, mouthing 'thank you' to him. Pastor Jim beamed with affirmation. Rosie then waved her thanks to each side of the aisle before taking her seat.

Rusty attempted to keep a vacant stare in her 'blind woman' role. But when she heard Rose's name and saw her face, she jerked in her seat almost blowing her cover. "What's Rosie doing here?" she said to no one in particular.

"That's Rosie?" the detective asked. "That makes things a little more complicated."

Rosie settled back onto the wooden seat and pulled the gold scarf around her shoulders to shield herself from the night's breeze. The sunset's rays bounced off the golden threads of her scarf sending a brilliant beam of light directly into J.D.'s eyes. All of a sudden, visions of the same scarf hugging a young redhead's hips over a decade before flooded his mind. He blinked twice and took a second look at the girl with the gold scarf. Lustful images of that gold scarf working its magic on him. Entreating. Beckoning. Seducing....

Am I losing my mind? J.D. shuddered and shook his head from side to side to clear his mind. Rubbing his eyes, he gazed over the crowd and zeroed in on the redhead in the fifth row. The familiarity he'd felt earlier brought a flicker of recognition. Then his heart stopped. The redhead glared at him with darts of loathing. He remembered the letter he'd destroyed the year before. Its raw words still festered in his mind and burned like fire from hell. *You killed her Jon.* It sent tremors through his soul and struck him hard, like a knife burning through his heart. Another image emerged of the gold scarf around a teenage mother holding a toddler on her hips. She had confronted him ten years before in a tent meeting such as this. He glanced down at the young girl sitting on the front row–the lame girl with black curly hair like his and the smile and the gold scarf of her mother's.

She's yours, Jon. Her name is Rose. His soul turned frigid. *That crippled girl is Rose–my daughter.* He felt the double-edged sword pierce his soul. His decrepit past had finally caught up with him. He trembled in his seat. It was time to pay his dues.

49 – REVELATION

Pastor Jim greeted the people, thanked them for coming, and then turned to introduce the evangelist. The arrogant countenance of the 'famous' preacher now had the captive look of a wild animal ready to claw its way out of a cage. Pastor Jim sent a silent prayer up for God's help. "Before turning the service over to our evangelist, I want to pray again for God's Hand on this service."

Blacart sat with his head in his hands, distracted by his own past. He only caught the last few words.

"Thank you, Father, for your sacrificial love. A love so great that You gave Your only Son so we could be in heaven with You someday. Help us see the truth tonight, Lord. Open the blinded eyes. Let people find real healing for their souls. Amen. And now, Reverend Blacart, the stage is yours."

Instead of jumping up and grabbing the microphone like so many nights before, J.D. rose slowly from his seat and made his way to the pulpit. As the men passed each other, Pastor Jim tapped J.D. on the shoulder and whispered. "Tonight is *your* night, J.D."

J.D. suddenly felt tired and weary. Weary of travel and weary of the game-playing. Meetings were exhilarating but exhausting. *I've nothing to show for my money. I've spent every penny on wine, women, and wild living. No home. No savings. No family. Everything's gone... and for what?*

His eyes darted to each tent exit, surveyed the expectant crowd, and counted in his head how many steps it would take to reach his motorhome. He then turned toward Pastor Jim. "I think the good pastor has already preached the sermon through his prayer."

Pastor Jim caught his wife's eye as he sat down on the platform. Mary nodded, put her hands together and bowed her head. Pastor Jim bowed his head and prayed silently.

J.D. put down the microphone and clicked his lapel mike on to have freedom with his hands. *The show will go on. Now, how can I spin this?*

With great flair, he bent low with arms opened wide toward the audience. Turning his face upward, he shouted. "Many are here tonight for a special blessing."

The crowd cheered.

He waved his hand over the right-hand side of the crowd, his glance landing on the 'blind' actress in the fifth row. "Blinded eyes *will* see."

Cheers exploded.

"Many will walk!" He pointed toward actors on the left. "And some deaf ears will hear!"

The people responded with thunderous applause.

"And, ladies and gentlemen," J.D. looked directly at Rusty. "Some will face their demons." An involuntary shudder racked his body.

"Something's changed," Flanders whispered to Rusty. "This is new."

"I feel it too," she said. "Not as flashy as usual. What's up?"

"Blacart seems unnerved."

"He'd better not run." She stared vacantly forward.

"He's changing things. Be ready to improvise if necessary."

"Oh, believe me. I already am," she said.

Blacart put his finger to his temple and closed his eyes. Then waving his finger over the crowd, he pretended to contemplate the recipient of his golden hand. He zeroed in on the redhead in the fifth row and pointed.

"Madam," he spoke so loud his mike screeched, "the lady with the red hair in the fifth row. Come to the front. Tonight, is YOUR night." He beckoned her to the platform as people clapped and cheered.

Flanders put his arm around Rusty and whispered in her ear. "Here we go."

"Now? Aren't we third in line?"

"Now," he said. As he rose, his plainclothesmen received their cue to move toward the front.

Flanders helped Rusty to her feet with great theatrics and then slipped his arm under hers. She tapped the cane back and forth, keeping her eyes straight ahead. With little steps, Flanders guided Rusty slowly to the platform and then moved off to the side. At the last moment, he discreetly flipped his camera to video-mode and aimed it toward the pulpit.

"Madam," J.D. declared, "tonight, you will regain your sight."

The closer Rusty came, the clearer J.D.'s recognition became. With her face away from the crowd, Rusty opened her eyes wide and stared at J.D.

She leaned to within inches of his face. The muscles of her neck were taut, her voice strained and raspy. "Remember me?" She scowled.

Blacart's face turned white. *My demon is here.*

50- ACCUSATIONS

Nina? Here? Rosie blinked her eyes and took a second look. *What's she doing up there? Nina's not blind.* She gave Pastor Jim a questioning look, but he looked like he was praying. Mary, who sat beside her, had her head bowed too. Rosie scratched her head. *What's going on?* She turned in her seat to search for Faith, who sat in the crowd. She found her sitting a few seats behind.

"It's Nina," she mouthed, hoping Faith could read her lips as she pointed to the lady up front. She held out her hands with palms up in alarm. Faith nodded her understanding and put her hands together in prayer form.

Rosie turned back toward the front, her eyes glued to the platform. *Nina, what are you doing?* A nasty sick knot settled in the pit of her stomach.

"Remember the letter, Jon?" Rusty asked, her mouth twisted into a snarl. "I promised to expose you as a fraud and a devil of deceit!" She glared at him.

J.D. took a step back. His lapel mike had picked up every word.

"You killed my daughter," her voice sounded like a

hiss. "Your sins have come home to roost."

Rosie couldn't understand. *What does Nina mean?*

The crowd became uneasy listening to the interchange and began whispering amongst themselves. Pastor Jim wiped the sweat from his brow. Glancing up, he saw the police officers close in toward the front, awaiting Flanders's cue to pounce. Although the night air was cool, his body was soaked with perspiration.

Blacart stared at Rusty but said nothing. Wanting the show to go on and avoid conflict, he feigned recognition as he had done with Carmen so many years before. Ignoring her rant, he pulled the vial of oil from his pocket, dabbed some on his finger, and reached to rub her eyes. She reared back.

"You will not touch me, mister!" She blocked her eyes from his hand.

Infuriated, J.D.'s gaze turned into a scowl. "Play your part, woman." He forgot his lapel mike was broadcasting it all.

He tried to tip her chin, but Rusty reared back so he couldn't touch her. She spun around to face the crowd. She was there to do one thing: Expose him. Defrock him. Take him down. "This man—" Rusty pointed at Blacart and began the speech she'd practiced so many times in her head.

Things were getting out of hand. Pastor Jim stood

to mediate, but the detective motioned with his hand to stand down. Pastor Jim grimaced and sat back down, rocking in place, praying inaudibly.

Rusty tried again. "I was never blind—" She screamed into the mike. Scanning the people for other actors from the night before she yelled, "Remember Mrs. Murphy?" Her finger pointed to the prim, white-haired lady sitting near the front. "She was never lame. And Hank James over there?" Rusty pointed out the burly man on the other side of the aisle. "He wasn't paralyzed. They were both putting on an act."

But her voice was drowned out by the noise of the crowd.

Throwing her cane down, she threw her hands in the air in frustration and wildly surveyed the crowd. Then her eyes landed on Rosie. Their eyes met, and for one moment, Rusty wished things could have been different.

"Look!" Someone shouted over the din. "She can see! J.D.'s healed her!"

"I WAS NEVER BLIND!" She screamed into the mike again.

Blacart grabbed Rusty's arm and swung her back around to face him. With his other palm, he pushed hard on her forehead. Rusty taunted him, stared him down, stood her ground, and refused to fall. The noise quieted as people watched the action before them.

"Make this look good," he warned.

"You're a phony, Jon," Rusty spit back. "I will not play any part in your mockery."

Blacart's evil black eyes burned fire into her skull. "Fall down, woman, for your own good." His forceful shove made her stumble backward.

The people gasped as Rusty screamed in defiance. "NOooooo!"

Losing her footing, the woman began to fall backward, struggling to keep her balance.

"Nina!" Rosie shot from her chair in a muddle of confusion, wanting to help her estranged grandmother. Without thinking of her bad leg, she tried to run toward the woman who had treated her with contempt for over ten years. Somehow that didn't matter to her anymore.

Stumbling over her own feet, she twisted her ankle on the uneven ground, sending her sprawling to the dirt. She lunged forward with her hands breaking her fall and protecting her face. As her knees came down with a thud, a jolt of power raced through Rosie's body. She froze in place, unsure of what just happened.

Blacart's wicked heart mellowed for a moment seeing his newfound daughter stumble. But when he began to move toward her, he was knocked backwards to the rough wooden platform by the same powerful force of electricity in the air. His face turned ashen as he flicked his hands to rid himself of the mighty current going through him.

Embarrassed, Rosie eased back on her legs and brushed the dirt from her hands and dress. She turned her head to search for Nina who had slunk back to her front-row seat. Then she looked for someone to help her up.

Pastor Jim rushed to the girl's side from his seat on the platform. He wrapped his arms around her. "Are you hurt, Rosie? Can you stand?"

She looked up at him with confusion, still dazed but with a wonderful feeling of safety in his arms.

The tent air was humid, but the atmosphere held more than moisture. The Spirit of God filled the place like a thick cloud settling over the masses. People sat on the edge of their seats with prickly skin, mouths agape as the scene unfolded in front of them. The whole place was energized with unseen forces.

Pastor Jim gently lifted the girl from her knees to her feet. As she put her weight on her bad leg, Rosie felt the awesome healing power of God fill her entire being. She bent to touch her leg as it tingled with warmth and her face began to glow like an angel. Balancing herself by holding onto Pastor Jim's arm, she stood on her good leg while holding the other out in front of her body.

People oohed as they witnessed her crooked leg

straighten and grow. Gasps of awe and cries of amazement emanated from onlookers. Then, as she stood on both legs tall and straight, a holy hush filled the tent.

"Oh, GOD! Thank You!" She shouted, raising her hands up high in praise. "My leg! It's healed!"

Then the shouting began. Hallelujahs and praise-the-Lords rang out with high praise to God as people rose to their feet, jumping up and down with their hands in the air.

Rosie stood on her tiptoes and spun in a full circle, a thrill of joy coursing through her being. She took off and ran, giggling all the way to the back of the tent as heaven's delight filled her heart. Her joyful laugh was contagious, and a dynamic surge of power spread through the people as they rejoiced with her, clapping and shouting praises to God.

"Look at me!" she cried as she passed Faith. Rosie lifted her face to the sky. "Look at me, Hope! Thank you, God! You really did it!"

Blacart, still buzzing and dazed, rubbed his eyes. "What just happened?"

51- TRUTH

"What just happened?" Pastor Jim ridiculed the stricken preacher. "God 'just happened'. Tonight, God's *real* Spirit came." He picked up the microphone and held up his hand to get the attention of the crowd.

"TONIGHT," he gave a long pause to allow the noise to quiet down. "Tonight, has been YOUR night," he declared to the people. "Instead of praising a man for his parlor tricks, you've seen the truly miraculous power of God. You have rightfully praised GOD and seen His wondrous works."

Rising to their feet again, people broke out with shouts of passionate praise and applause. After a long burst of worship, Pastor Jim motioned for them to sit once more.

"What you have seen all week has not been miracles from the Lord. It has been the deception of this man, J.D. Blacart: a master trickster." He pointed to the shamed preacher, still in shock on his knees, his hands over his eyes. "Through smoke and mirrors, he's betrayed you. He has paid performers to stage phony acts and then led you to believe God worked wonders through his hands. He had everyone blinded and fooled, including himself. He believed a lie, and that lie became his life. Everything he did was justified in his own eyes. Although he preached peace and love, he could not find it himself."

Still kneeling, J.D. moved his hands to his head, and then bowed to put his head between his knees. Detective John Flanders flicked off his video camera and walked over to Blacart. Pulling him to his feet, Flanders's words were heard through J.D.'s still-live lapel mike. "J.D. Blacart, you're under arrest for duplicitous behavior with intent to commit fraud, swindling, and larceny. You can go with me quietly, or I'll put the cuffs on you and drag you out of here in front of everyone."

"I'll go willingly," Blacart surrendered in defeat. "I've been caught. But first, I have a few last words. Would you walk me to the pulpit?"

Pastor Jim stepped aside as Flanders guided J.D. Blacart beside the pulpit. The detective and the pastor exchanged curious glances. A look of compassion for this self-made man who suddenly looked very small showed on Pastor's Jim's countenance.

Blacart hung his head in resignation to a long-awaited consequence. The once-flamboyant man now stood in front of the crowd speechless, as words refused to come. The silence grew deafening. Every eye was on the once-wild preacher. He heaved a heavy sigh that sounded like his last. Finally, he spoke.

"It's true. I'm not the man you thought I was," he confessed. "All my life has been shrouded with trickery and deceit—one big scam. I've put on good shows–but that's all they were. I made a name for myself, but it was not a name to be proud of. I began this service by saying we would face our demons. Tonight, I faced mine." J.D. choked. "My past has now met me face to face. I faked it all. I admit it. I don't know if I ever really believed in God or His power–until tonight when I too witnessed God's real healing power. It had nothing to do with me... it was all Him."

Loud gasps were heard throughout the tent. People began to murmur among themselves, asking questions, making comments. Women put their hands over their mouths as men wagged their heads pointing accusations at the defamed man.

"Pastor Jim said I've justified everything in my own eyes, and...," he sighed loud and long. "He's right. My eyes have been lustful and proud." J.D. turned his face toward Pastor Jim with a vacant stare. "And tonight, the same Power I've mocked for years has struck me blind."

"Serves you right, Blacart," yelled out Rusty. Murmurs arose once more.

J.D. hung his head in humiliation. "I'm ready now." He held out his hands.

Flanders put his hand on the man's shoulder and led him off the platform where the other officers cuffed him and led him away. The detective then walked over and sat down beside Rusty on the front row. "You've fulfilled your part of the plea deal. And thanks to you, we've taken this charlatan down. Now, are you ready to pay your debt?" Flanders whispered to her.

Rusty gave Rosie one last glance across the aisle and then nodded. "Serves me right," she said.

52–UNEXPECTED MIRACLES

Ushers began to roll wheelchairs out as people got up to leave. Pastor Jim spoke into the mike again. "Before you all leave, I want to give you one last word of encouragement. Maybe it will strengthen your faith, too."

The people stopped and turned to listen.

"When we first set up these meetings, we never dreamed how it would turn out. Sometimes God provides miracles in ways you don't expect. It may be instantaneous like Rose just experienced." He looked down at Rosie and smiled. "Or, sometimes, it takes time. Never stop believing in God's goodness. He always knows the best time for your miracle to come to pass." Pastor Jim looked at his wife sitting on the front and held his hand out to her. "Mary? Come join me on the platform."

When Mary reached her husband, he whispered something in her ear. She nodded with a wide smile. Pastor Jim took Mary's hands in his. "And sometimes, God provides a miracle in a completely practical way, like He did for us. We've wanted a child for a long time but were never able to conceive. So, we've fostered babies and toddlers for a few years. This past year we took a step of faith and accepted an older child–Rose, our foster daughter."

People began to clap until Pastor Jim held up his hand again. "Rose, come join us." He beckoned her with his hand.

She walked up to the platform without a limp, straight and tall. Mary welcomed her with outstretched arms.

"We've come to love Rose like our own. And soon, we'll have her for real. Rose, we are going to adopt you. The paperwork is already started."

Rosie's eyes widened. She flung her hands over her heart to stop it from beating out of her chest. "Really?"

He nodded with a big grin.

She threw her arms around them both and squeezed tight. Lifting her face towards the sky, she shouted. "Another miracle! Thank you, God! A real mom and dad!" Huge, wet tears of gratitude splashed down her shiny cheeks.

"We're a real family now." Pastor Jim whispered in her ear through a lump in his throat. He cupped her face in his hands and wiped away her tears with his fingers.

Rosie's face began to feel warmer and tighter and then began to tingle with pins and needles. She peered up into Pastor Jim's eyes with wonder. "I think God's done it again." She whispered to him in awe.

He removed his hands, and she ran her finger over

her cheek. Only a tiny spot remained where the jagged scar once ran. She turned and faced the crowd. "Praise be to God forever! He's done it again!" Tilting her head to the sky, she shouted, "the devil's kiss is gone!"

Mary smoothed Rosie's hair away from her cheek. "And all that remains is a tiny rose-colored heart! God has kissed away your pain." Mary put her arm around Rosie's waist. "And now you truly have God's beauty mark of honor."

The volcano of applause erupted once more as the crowd witnessed the tender scene. People raised their hands and heads toward heaven in praise and thanksgiving.

Pastor Jim turned toward the crowd that didn't want to leave. His heart was full; his soul was thankful. "Praise be to God forever!"

"Praise be to God forever!" They repeated in unison.

"So, go with God. Watch and pray so you won't be deceived. Live in God's presence every day because you never know when it might be YOUR day for God's surprise. If you look for them, YOUR miracle might be right around the corner!"

WHERE
THERE IS
HOPE
THERE IS
FAITH
WHERE THERE
IS FAITH
MIRACLES
HAPPEN

EPILOGUE

J.D. Blacart was convicted in a court of law and sentenced to twenty years in federal prison because of larceny, swindling, and fraud. He is currently dictating his book on *The Art of Deception: The Expose of a Swindler*.

~ ~ ~ ~ ~

Rusty Delahunt, also known as Rozlyn Delahunt Gavotte, also known as Nina, failed all classes on anger management. Stripped of all parental rights by the court, she is currently serving prison time for child endangerment, child abuse, abandonment, child neglect, and prostitution.

As part of Rusty's plea deal, "Benny's Place" was closed after Detective John Flanders raided the place for prostitution later that fall. Benny was convicted and sent to prison.

~ ~ ~ ~ ~

After Pastor Jim and Mary Davis adopted Rose Delahunt, Mary discovered she was pregnant with their first child. They continue to pastor the little church on Shepherd's Creek Road near Ridgetown, Missouri, where Faith Abrams still faithfully attends. Pastor Jim vows to never sponsor another evangelistic tent meeting.

~ ~ ~ ~ ~

Overjoyed to have real parents, Rose Delahunt-Davis was ecstatic when she learned she would have a little sister. After finishing high school, she went on to study music at Sunshine Music Academy in east Missouri, thankful for a full four-year scholarship from her Grandfather Raymond Gavotte. She majored in classical piano and followed her passion for ballet. She visits her grandmother monthly in jail and performs mini concerts for her Grandfather Gavotte at the senior residential home whenever she can.

She was never told J.D. Blacart was her father.

-The End-

A Word from the Author

Writing has been a love of my life since I was a child. Although close to 400 nonfiction articles had been written and published nation-wide, writing fiction didn't evolve until my children were grown, When I joined the local writers' group, I received the encouragement needed to spin true stories into fiction and create new fiction of my own.

My goal in writing is to find a theme that motivates, encourages, inspires, or provokes the reader to thought. My novels are written with family in mind with drama, adventure, romance, with a little mystery thrown in. With every book or story, the reader is left with a good moral principle to live by. *RUNAWAY* is the fourth novel since 2013.

Beginning in 2016, I began to use my computer skills to assist other aspiring authors. As a former I.T. teacher, this comes easy and is fun for me to format their books, design their covers and see their dreams come true. If you would like my assistance, please contact me.

Candy Simonson

Contact me: casimonson@hotmail.com
WEBSITE: http://www.casimonson.com
Like me: http://www.facebook.com/casimonson

OTHER BOOKS BY C.A. SIMONSON

Available on Amazon.com in print, digital, and audio.

Contemporary Christian Family Fiction

"The Journey Home Series"- written in "Little House" style

LOVE'S JOURNEY HOME - Seven children, abandoned by their drunken father, must separate to survive. Frank tried to escape his past, but it followed him. Then he met Anne – and she changed everything. Follow Frank as he journeys from a boy into manhood.

LOVE LOOKS BACK - Anne convinces Frank to go back home. Look for his lost siblings. What he finds is a murder in the barn. A cross out back marks his pa's grave. Did his oldest brother kill him? Frank must prove his brother's innocence.

LOVE'S AMAZING GRACE - Convinced he killed his father, the eldest brother runs away to join the Navy during WWII. Now he finds himself on a sinking ship in the middle of the ocean, abandoned again. He'll make any promise if God will get him out of this mess.

DISCOVER OR ORDER OTHER BOOKS:

http://www.amazon.com/author/casimonson

If you've enjoyed this book, please take a moment to write a review on Amazon or GoodReads.com. Simply go to where the book is sold, scroll to the bottom, and type in your thoughts.

FOOD HACKS, HELPS, HINTS has over 350 tips on selecting food, preparing it quicker and easier, and making it taste better! PLUS, over 250 extra ways on using food for beauty or cleaning. That's not all! Lots of fun food trivia and facts throughout.

Perfect for the newbie in the kitchen or the seasoned pro!

Thoughts for Evening Time: Devotions to Ponder

Get Hope. Be Encouraged. Settle Your Mind.

Faith is built in layers. When a seed of hope is planted, faith grows. God proves His unfailing faithfulness as we learn to trust. Read daily nuggets of truth and hope for an unstable and insecure world.

Available on Amazon.com
...or read for FREE
with Kindle Unlimited

99¢

Click links or books to buy from Amazon

THE CHRISTMAS ADVENTURE

A short fuzzy Christmas story on the love of giving

A QUICK READ

58 SHORT-SHORT STORIES written in 26 sentences from A-Z

Romance/Sci-Fi/Drama/and more

ALL BEAUTIFUL CREATURES
Story Coloring Book

For the kiddos – a primer, a storybook, and a coloring book of amazing animals of the world.

Made in the USA
Monee, IL
23 September 2021